Sara.

From the first time Lucas had seen her, he'd known she couldn't be Analise, because Analise had never turned his brain to mush while sending his hormones skyrocketing.

Okay, he was attracted to Sara. Very attracted. And he liked her. Admired her. Respected her. Wanted to take care of her and make her happy.

But he wasn't in love.

He couldn't be in love.

He refused to be in love.

But every time he closed his eyes, Sara's face appeared. And no matter how hard he tried to convince himself it was really Analise's face, he didn't believe himself.

Dear Reader,

In May 2000 Silhouette Romance will commemorate its twentieth anniversary! This line has always celebrated the essence of true love in a manner that blends classic themes and the challenges of romance in today's world into a reassuring, fulfilling novel. From the enchantment of first love to the wonder of second chance, a Silhouette Romance novel demonstrates the power of genuine emotion and the breathless connection that develops between a man and a woman as they discover each other. And this month's stellar selections are quintessential Silhouette Romance stories!

If you've been following LOVING THE BOSS, you'll be amazed when mysterious Rex Barrington III is unmasked in *I Married the Boss!* by Laura Anthony. In this month's FABULOUS FATHERS offering by Donna Clayton, a woman discovers *His Ten-Year-Old Secret*. And opposites attract in *The Rancher and the Heiress,* the third of Susan Meier's TEXAS FAMILY TIES miniseries.

WRANGLERS & LACE returns with Julianna Morris's *The Marriage Stampede*. In this appealing story, a cowgirl butts heads—and hearts—with a bachelor bent on staying that way. Sally Carleen unveils the first book in her exciting duo ON THE WAY TO A WEDDING… with the tale of a twin mistaken for an M.D.'s *Bride in Waiting!* It's both a blessing and a dilemma for a single mother when she's confronted with an amnesiac *Husband Found,* this month's FAMILY MATTERS title by Martha Shields.

Enjoy the timeless power of Romance this month, and every month—you won't be disappointed!

Mary-Theresa Hussey

Mary-Theresa Hussey
Senior Editor, Silhouette Romance

Please address questions and book requests to:
Silhouette Reader Service
U.S.: 3010 Walden Ave., P.O. Box 1325, Buffalo, NY 14269
Canadian: P.O. Box 609, Fort Erie, Ont. L2A 5X3

A BRIDE
IN WAITING

Sally Carleen

Silhouette
ROMANCE™
Published by Silhouette Books
America's Publisher of Contemporary Romance

For Lynda Powell Cilwick,
who believed in Sara long before I did.

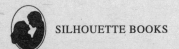 SILHOUETTE BOOKS

ISBN 0-373-19376-9

A BRIDE IN WAITING

Copyright © 1999 by Sally B. Steward

This edition published by arrangement with Harlequin Books S.A.

® and TM are trademarks of Harlequin Books S.A., used under license.
Trademarks indicated with ® are registered in the United States Patent
and Trademark Office, the Canadian Trade Marks Office and in other
countries.

Look us up on-line at: http://www.romance.net

Printed in U.S.A.

Books by Sally Carleen

Silhouette Romance

An Improbable Wife #1101
Cody's Christmas Wish #1124
My Favorite Husband #1183
Porcupine Ranch #1221
With This Child... #1281
*A Bride in Waiting #1376

*On the Way to a Wedding...

Silhouette Shadows

Shaded Leaves of Destiny #46

SALLY CARLEEN,

the daughter of a cowboy and a mail-order bride, has romance in her genes. Factor in the grandfather in 1890s Louisiana who stole the crowd at political rallies by standing on a flatbed wagon and telling stories, and it's no surprise she ended up writing romance novels.

Sally, a hard-core romantic who expects life and novels to have happy endings, is married to Max Steward, and they live in Lee's Summit, Missouri, with their large cat, Leo, and their very small dog, Cricket. Her hobbies are drinking Coca-Cola and eating chocolate, especially Ben & Jerry's Phish Food ice cream. Sally loves to hear from her readers; P.O. Box 6614, Lee's Summit, MO 64064.

The honor of your presence

is requested at the marriage of

~~Miss Analise Brewster~~ Sara Martin???

to

Dr. Lucas Daniels

Saturday, the twelfth of June

at two o'clock

Grand Avenue Methodist Church

Briar Creek, Texas

Chapter One

Steam hissed from under the hood of Lucas Daniels's silver Mercedes.

Muttering a curse, he slammed a fist against the steering wheel then yanked the traitor of a car to the side, into a parking space on Main Street—smack in the middle of downtown Briar Creek, Texas, on a Saturday afternoon.

Great. He could get out right here and make an announcement to the whole town rather than waiting for them to hear it via the gossip line. Skip the middleman. Maybe the news would travel fast enough that he wouldn't have to be the one to tell his future in-laws, who were doubtless waiting at the church.

Analise Brewster will not be attending her own wedding rehearsal because she has skipped town. Make that *skipped town, exclamation point* since Analise's note announcing that fact oozed exclamation points. And why not? She talked in exclamation points.

Both Lucas and Analise's father, Ralph, had thought

marriage would curb her impulsiveness, bring out a sense of responsibility, but so far the engagement hadn't done much in that direction.

Her parents, especially her mother, were going to be very upset, as they always were when she got out of their sight for longer than a few minutes. They were overly protective and Analise was overly independent, a bad combination.

With another vehement curse, he climbed out into the east Texas summer day. The June sun beat down from above while heat rose from the street in waves to assault him from below. Though at this point he really couldn't tell how much of that heat came from the sun and how much from his own anger.

He reached for the hood and burned his fingers on the hot metal. "Damn!" He bit back the rest of the litany of swearwords he'd have liked to run through.

A big hand clapped him on the back. "Got a problem, Lucas, my boy?"

My boy. After six years of practice, he was still a boy, still the *new* doctor…still Wayne Daniels's son, accepted only because Ralph Brewster had taken him into his established practice. This new scandal wasn't likely to increase anybody's confidence in him.

Lucas turned toward the smiling face. "You could say that, Herb."

"Need a ride somewhere?"

Lucas plowed his fingers through his hair. He might as well tell Herb the truth and get it over with. Briar Creek was a small town. If, by chance, there was one person here that he didn't know, Analise's family did. Soon everybody would know about Analise's latest escapade.

"Yeah," he said. "Thanks. I could use a ride to the Methodist church over on Grand."

"Getting ready for that big wedding, huh? I just saw Analise walking down Wyandotte."

"What?"

Herb chuckled. "Reckon she's gonna be late to your shindig, like she's late to everything else. That's our Analise."

Lucas grabbed Herb's arm. "Just now? You saw her just now?"

"Well, as long ago as it took me to drive one block. I wasn't driving very fast, of course. I'm not in any hurry."

"Which direction was she going?"

Herb pointed up the street. "That way."

Lucas whirled and charged in the direction Herb indicated. "Thanks!" he said over his shoulder.

"You still need that ride?"

"I'll get Analise to take me." *After I kill her.*

As he strode along the sidewalk, Lucas forced himself to smile and greet everybody he met, pretend nothing was wrong. He turned at the corner and went toward Wyandotte, the next street over, resisting the impulse to run, to catch his flaky fiancée quickly before she did something else crazy.

"Good afternoon, Mrs. Greene. How's Willie's rheumatism?"

"Better, Lucas. Nice to see you. Tell Analise I said hello."

He turned onto Wyandotte and there she was, staring into the window of Fulton's Antiques.

Lucas clenched his teeth as he strode toward her. What kind of game was she playing, sending him a note telling him she was leaving town, then putting on those frumpy clothes, pulling her hair back in that braid and going downtown? Did she think she was disguised? Tall and willowy with that red hair and those distinctive features—large eyes, wide forehead and straight, patrician nose—it would take more than a change of clothes and hairstyle to disguise Analise Brewster.

She didn't even look up as he approached.

"What do you think you're doing?" he demanded.

Sara Martin flinched at the angry tone in the man's voice, but he couldn't be talking to her. Someone else was in trouble this time.

She turned her back to the sound and started to continue down the street, anxious to avoid whatever scene was about to occur.

The man grabbed her arm. "Analise!"

She gasped, whirling to face her attacker, automatically bringing her knee up to his groin then smashing her heel into his instep. The heel of her hand went toward his nose, but she stopped herself as he released her, gave a strangled groan and sank to his knees on the sidewalk.

She gaped at the man in shock. "Omigosh! It worked!" She reached toward him to help him up, then recalled herself and stepped backward.

She'd always thought her mother was a little paranoid the way she constantly forced her to practice self-defense techniques, to be prepared to get away from a potential attacker and run. But now she'd actually been attacked, and she'd freed herself and she was standing on the sidewalk of a strange town, thinking she ought to help her attacker instead of running for her life. She had the actions right, but the attitude had gotten off track somewhere.

The man didn't look dangerous. However, in his

khaki slacks and white knit shirt with a little animal embroidered on one side, his black hair immaculately cut and styled, he did look exactly like the kind of man her mother had always taught her to fear—sophisticated, worldly, possibly wealthy.

Even so, the exasperated expression mingling with the pain in his brown eyes kept her rooted in place. That and the equally exasperated tone in his voice when he once again called her by the name of her favorite childhood doll as he struggled to his feet.

"Damn it, Analise, why'd you do that? What in heaven's name are you up to? Did you think wearing that frumpy dress and pulling your hair back would disguise you? Have you gone completely nuts?"

Frumpy? She'd made this dress herself. Maybe she ought to kick him again.

Taking a couple more steps backward, she fumbled in her purse then withdrew her pepper spray. "Look, mister, either you're the one who's nuts, or you've mistaken me for somebody else. My name is not Analise. It's—" She hesitated, the old fears surfacing, fears her mother had drilled into her head all her life. *Never talk to strangers. Never tell anyone your name or my name or where we live.* She pointed the spray at him. "It's not Analise," she finished. "I'm leaving now, and you'd better not try to stop me, or I'll use this."

The tendons stood out on the man's neck, and the muscles clenched in his tanned, square jaw, a jaw out of sync with the perfect clothes and hairstyle. "Analise, this isn't funny."

A small, birdlike woman with curly blue hair came up from behind the man, stopped, smiled and wagged a finger. "Why, Analise and Lucas! What are you two naughty lovebirds doing here when you're supposed to be at your wedding rehearsal?''

Either the whole town was crazy, or she really did look like this Analise. Which could mean—

Her heart skipped a beat then went into an erratic rhythm as she thought of the implications of another woman looking so much like her.

"Hello, Mrs. Wilson," the man said smoothly. "I guess we just lost track of time. We're on our way right now."

No, it couldn't be. If Analise was her biological mother, she'd be too old to be marrying this Lucas person. Unless he liked older women. Or her mother had had a face-lift.

"I can't wait to see that wedding gown, Analise. Eleanor told me it's the prettiest thing she ever made." She looked at Sara's loose cotton dress and frowned, then changed it back to a smile. "Of course, you look beautiful in anything. Even with your hair pulled back like that. Though I like it better all loose and curly. Don't you, Lucas?"

The man she called Lucas lifted the long braid off her back and stared at it curiously. "Yes, I do," he said, his hand moving along the length of the braid then up to her head, his touch exploratory and surprisingly gentle.

Sara sucked in her breath, fighting fear and confusion. She wanted to bolt away from these two people who called her by the name of a doll, from this man who shouldn't be touching her so familiarly and from her own unexpected pleasure at that touch.

"You kids get on to the church now, you hear?"

"We will, Mrs. Wilson." Lucas's voice was strangely subdued, the anger and exasperation in his dark eyes replaced by confusion as he spoke to Mrs. Wilson but looked directly at Sara.

"How did you get this thing attached so good?" he asked as Mrs. Wilson walked away.

"What thing? My hair?"

He continued to hold the braid with one hand. "It can't be your hair. Yesterday your hair was only shoulder length."

Sara swallowed hard and gripped the pepper spray tighter. Just in case. "I'm not your Analise," she said, the words coming out barely above a whisper. "I came to town this morning. I'm looking for...relatives. If your Analise looks so much like me, maybe she's my...relative."

Lucas said nothing, but his narrowed gaze and raised eyebrow showed his skepticism.

"Turn loose of my braid," she said breathlessly. "I'll take it down and show you how long my hair is. It comes to my waist. It's never been cut, never been shoulder length."

He didn't turn it loose. Instead, he pulled the band from the end and began to unwind the strands. She held her breath as he ran his fingers through the heavy mass of her hair, plunging them into its depths, over her scalp and down again.

Somehow the action seemed far too intimate for two strangers standing on a public street in the middle of the day.

No, she realized, not the action, but her reaction. Lucas's touch exploded her nerve endings, sending delectable sensations washing over her, making her wish he'd never stop.

She jerked away from him, her hair swirling about

her, out of his reach. "You see?" she asked breath-lessly. "I'm not Analise."

Lucas blinked against the sunlight as if suddenly awakened, one hand still outstretched to the space where her hair had been. His hand fell to his side. "No, you're not." His voice had a dusky quality that matched the look in his dark eyes. "You have her skin, her eyes, her lips…"

She stepped back before he could touch her again, before he could stir those sensations she didn't want stirred. "I need to go." She wasn't sure if she was talking to him or to herself or why she felt it necessary to say the words. He wasn't restraining her.

"Except for the way you wear your hair, you could be her twin, but you're not her."

"Her twin? I could be her twin?" Sara's mind whirled. Was that possible? Could her real mother have given birth to twins, and her adoptive mother only took one of the girls? Did she have a sister, a twin she'd never met who'd been adopted by someone here in Briar Creek?

She'd named her favorite doll Analise and pretended it was her sister. Had that been more then wishing? Twins were supposed to have that kind of sixth sense about each other, even when separated at birth.

"Is Analise your fiancée? Can I meet her? Please. It's very important."

He stared at her uncomprehendingly for a moment, then ran his fingers through his own hair, shook his head and laughed without humor.

"Yeah, she's my fiancée and, no, you can't meet her. I don't know where she is."

"You don't know where your fiancée is?"

He looked up and down the street as if checking to

see if anyone was watching, then shrugged and pulled a folded piece of pink paper from his pants pocket. "This was delivered to my house a few minutes ago, just as I was leaving to go to our wedding rehearsal."

Sara returned her pepper spray to her purse and examined the paper. "A flyer for twenty percent off on treating your lawn for grubworms?" Maybe the man was crazy after all.

"The other side." He reached across and flipped the paper over. The words leaped off the page, scrawled in a hasty, flowing script.

I have to leave town for a few days! Tell Mom and Dad I'll call them this evening! When I come back, I'll have some really big news! I know you'll understand that I absolutely had to go because you're my best friend in the whole world and you always understand me!

Hugs—Analise

P.S. By the way, you might want to postpone the wedding rehearsal for a few days!

Sara's heart sank. This couldn't be her sister, this person who wrote so exuberantly and ended every sentence with an exclamation point. This irresponsible person who deserted her fiancé on the day of their wedding rehearsal.

"I'm sorry," she said, handing the note back to him. He shrugged. "That's Analise."

"You mean she's done things like this before?"

"Not quite this bad. And not since we decided to get married. Her parents and I thought marriage might make her a little more dependable, but it looks like we were wrong.'' He stuffed the paper back into his pocket. ''I apologize for the mistake. You really do look like her.''

''Like her twin.''

''Yeah. Like her twin. Well.'' He shifted from one foot to the other, a nervous action at odds with his urbane appearance. ''I guess I might as well get on over to the church and face the music. So I'll leave you to whatever you were doing before I came along and interrupted.''

''Yes. Okay.''

He made no move to leave and neither did she. Sara felt oddly reluctant to part from Lucas. A natural reluctance since she desperately wanted to find out more about the missing Analise. It wasn't even partly because of the way Lucas had touched her hair or the way he was looking at her, as if he wanted to touch her again.

''Maybe you could tell me—''

''I have an idea—''

They both spoke at the same time.

He smiled. ''Go ahead. You first.''

''I just got to town a little while ago, and I'm trying to find some information about…missing members of my family. I don't know where to start.''

His eyes narrowed. ''You think because Analise looks like you, she may be a relative.''

''Maybe.'' She saw no reason to tell him everything.

He nodded slowly, assessingly. ''I'll make you a deal. I'll do my best to help you find your relatives if you'll help me for just a couple of hours.''

Sara gulped and fumbled for her pepper spray. ''What do you want me to do?''

''Analise will be back in a few days with some story of a new discovery, some new kind of a butterfly they've identified over in Dallas or something equally ridiculous.''

Sara's mouth went dry. ''A new species of butterfly? She's interested in butterflies?''

''Bugs. All kinds of bugs. She's a zoology major.''

''I wanted to major in zoology with a specialty in entomology! That's insects,'' she explained at Lucas's startled look.

''I know what it is. That's Analise's field, too.''

''Oh!'' She told herself she shouldn't become too excited; that could only lead to disappointment. Nevertheless the evidence was mounting. The evidence plus that odd feeling she'd always had about having a sister. Her mother had told her that was normal for only children, but she'd never quite believed her on that one.

''Be glad you didn't,'' he said, and for a moment Sara thought she must have spoken aloud, but he was responding to her comment about her frustrated desire to major in zoology. ''Analise hasn't had much luck finding a job in that field. Anyway, she'll be back in a few days and everybody will laugh and shake their heads because everybody loves her in spite of her flaky ways. But today her parents, who are wonderful people, are going to be very worried about her.''

He pulled the folded paper from his pocket again and regarded it balefully. ''There's no way we can reschedule the rehearsal. We made the wedding plans in a bit of a hurry. Analise couldn't make up her mind until the last minute. Now the wedding's set for next Saturday afternoon, squeezed in between one in the morning and another one in the late afternoon, and this is the only time we could get the church for rehearsal between now and then. This whole thing started out a mess, and it's getting worse.'' He looked directly into her eyes, his gaze so powerful, Sara felt her legs could turn to rubber and he'd still be able to hold her erect. "Unless you come to that rehearsal with me and pretend to be her."

"What? Pretend to be somebody else? I couldn't do that!"

"Sure you could. This is a rehearsal. All you have to do is whatever the coordinator tells you. I'll pay you. Fifty dollars an hour. A hundred dollars an hour."

She stared up at him, shocked and dismayed by the offer of money. In spite of her misgivings about pretending to be someone else, she'd wanted to agree until then, wanted to find out about this woman who looked so much like her.

But how many times had her mother warned her not to trust anyone with money? And illogical as she now knew such warnings, they were too deeply ingrained in her to ignore.

She shook her head slowly, a part of her still wanting to go with him, to take a chance for once in her life, to explore a path that might lead to a new identity for herself...to her real mother...or maybe, just possibly, to a sister.

"I'll help you find whatever information you need, and when Analise comes back, I'll make sure you get to meet her first thing."

He'd moved closer to her or she to him, so close she could smell his expensive cologne, a scent that didn't quite mask his own rugged, masculine essence.

"No," she whispered. "I can't."

His features softened and his hand lifted to her cheek, pushing her hair back from her face. Above her his lips moved, forming the word *please,* and she could almost feel those lips on hers.

Wicked! her mother would have said. *Dangerous!*

"Yes," Sara said.

Chapter Two

Sara clutched the steering wheel with one hand and the door handle with the other as she drove across town with Lucas in the car beside her, guiding her along the unfamiliar streets.

What on earth was she doing, going somewhere with a strange man, entering a strange world, pretending to be another woman? Was it possible this strange man could even turn out to be the kidnapper her mother had always feared?

The last notion was another holdover from her mother's paranoia, she tried to reassure herself. A kidnapper didn't approach his victim and ask her to pretend to be his bride.

Nevertheless, she was infinitely relieved when Lucas directed her into the parking lot of a huge stone church. Surely a kidnapper wouldn't take his victim to church first.

''Park over there,'' he said, indicating a far corner of

the lot, "so nobody will notice you're not driving Analise's car."

Sara's gaze swept the assortment of luxury automo-
biles directly in front of the church. Her ten-year-old
midsize sedan would certainly stand out in that company. "What kind of car does Analise have?"

He sighed and turned to her with a rueful grin. "A
fast one. A small, red sports car that enables our local
police force to write their quota of speeding tickets
every month."

A car that matched the handwriting on the note from
Analise.

"I've never knowingly exceeded the speed limit in
my life," Sara mused. "Where does she get the money
to pay all those tickets if she can't find a job?"

"Her parents have big bucks. Her father, Ralph
Brewster, is a doctor and her mother's family founded
this town."

That information didn't do anything to soothe Sara's
nerves. "I'm not sure I can do this, pretend to be someone so different."

Lucas's dark eyes scrutinized her face. He shook his
head and for one moment Sara feared he was going to
agree with her. In that moment she realized how desperately she wanted to do this, to find out more about
Analise, the woman who looked so much like her.

To prove to herself that she could do this.

"Different?" he said. "I can't get over how much
you two look alike. It's uncanny. If I didn't know better…well, trust me, you won't have any problems. All
you have to do is listen to the wedding coordinator.
She'll tell you everything in a voice you couldn't miss
if you were in the next county. Let's hurry. We're late."

They got out of the car and started across the lot

toward the church. If the situation wasn't bad enough, that church made it worse. It loomed ahead, big, old, solid and intimidating. The stained-glass windows seemed to watch her approach, daring such an inconsequential person as her to enter. She didn't belong in any place so grand. The church knew it and all the people inside would notice immediately.

"Wait a minute." Lucas's words stopped her. She whirled back toward him, irrational fear flooding her for just a moment. Surely a kidnapper wouldn't kidnap in a church parking lot. "We have to do something about your hair."

He reached around her for the braid she'd redone and tucked it into the collar of her dress.

"Your skin's cold," he said softly, his fingers lingering deliciously on the bare flesh of her neck.

She laughed nervously. "It's at least ninety degrees. I can't be cold." Though judging from the relative warmth of his touch, she knew she must be.

He jerked his hand away as though she had suddenly burned him. "Your skin's clammy," he said, his tone brisk and businesslike. "A typical reaction to stress. You're really nervous about this, aren't you?"

"I'm okay. Let's get this over with." She walked defiantly toward the church.

"Hey!"

She stopped again, one foot on the front step.

"I don't know your name or anything about you."

"Sara Martin. I'm a librarian. I'm from Deauxville, Missouri."

He smiled, and Sara's fears somehow vanished in that flash of white teeth against tanned skin, of his dark eyes lighting from within. "Hi, Sara Martin. I'm Lucas Daniels, and I'm a doctor from Briar Creek who's greatly in your debt.''

He took her hand and they went into the church, into the hushed atmosphere of a huge auditorium with burgundy carpet that sank beneath Sara's feet. Pews upholstered in velvet fabric of the same color sat in quiet, orderly rows. The place even smelled like burgundy velvet…rich and dignified and established.

The intimidating hush was shattered in the next second by a chaotic crowd of people bustling and shouting.

''Thank goodness you're here! We were getting worried.''

''Analise, can't you ever be on time?''

''Analise, my dress hasn't come in yet!''

''Will everyone please settle down so we can get started here.''

Sara took an instinctive step backward and felt Lucas's strong hands on her shoulders, supporting her and urging her forward.

''It's all right,'' he murmured, his voice deep and reassuring in her ear.

''The bride and her attendants stay at the back. I need the groom and his attendants here,'' a slim, elegant woman standing to one side up front directed, and Lucas left Sara.

Three laughing, confident young women converged on her instead, and Sara shrank inside.

''Cool hair,'' a brown-eyed blonde said. ''Makes you look sophisticated. Kind of like a real wife.''

''Cool dress, too,'' a short brunette added. ''Wish I could carry off that look. On me, it'd just be dowdy.''

What was it with these people and her dress?

''Quiet, everyone,'' the authoritative woman ordered. Obviously she was the coordinator Lucas had mentioned. "The minister, the groom and his attendants will enter from the front and stand looking to the back, waiting for the bride."

As the men, including Lucas, moved solemnly into their places, the whole thing took on a dreamlike quality.

"Marilyn sings the solo, then as soon as the organist begins to play, Judy starts down the aisle. When she's halfway, Kathy starts, then Linda. Okay, pretend the solo's just finished. Nancy, begin the music." Strains of organ music floated through the auditorium. "Judy, start down the aisle. As soon as you get to the front, turn and face the back, all attention focusing on the bride. Stop giggling, Judy, and, for goodness' sake, don't be chewing gum during the actual wedding."

One by one, the three women moved down the aisle, leaving Sara alone with everyone staring at her.

Lucas had been wrong. She'd been wrong. She couldn't do this, couldn't pull off something so daring as masquerading as another woman. The most daring thing she'd ever done before was...well, the only daring thing she'd ever done was sell everything after her mother's death and come to Briar Creek, Texas. And right now she regretted that, big time.

She half turned to run from the church, get in her car and go back to Deauxville, forget all about finding her real mother or this unlikely possibility of a twin sister.

But a tall, portly man moved up beside her and, smiling down at her, took her arm, and she was mesmerized by the total acceptance and love in his eyes. The organist broke into the strains of the wedding march.

"Okay, bride, you're on. This is your show. Take it slow and graceful. Do *not* run down the aisle."

The tall man winked. "My baby girl went straight

from crawling to running. What makes that woman think you're going to change now?''

Analise's father.

The love that emanated from him was for his daughter, not for her.

But it was so hard not to luxuriate in the paternal adoration, something she'd never experienced before.

In a daze she walked down the aisle beside Analise's devoted father, moving toward Lucas, Analise's beaming groom. It was hard to fight the urge to become lost in the pretense, to believe she really was Analise Brewster, beloved daughter and fiancée, the person who belonged in this church, in this community, in this wedding.

''Who gives this woman in marriage?''

''Her mother and I.''

The older man placed her hand in Lucas's. He gave her a conspiratorial smile, and she could no longer resist becoming hopelessly lost in the wedding fantasy.

''The minister reads the vows. You each answer 'I do' and exchange rings.''

''I do,'' Sara whispered, holding her hand out for Lucas to slip on the invisible ring, then doing the same for him.

''Then you kiss the bride, turn to face the congregation, and the minister introduces you as Mr. and Mrs. Lucas Daniels.''

Lucas's dark gaze held hers for an instant then dropped to her lips. As if in slow motion, his face lowered toward hers, his lips touching hers gently, possessively, lighting unexpected fires inside her while promising a lifetime of love and belonging. For that brief moment she almost believed that promise was for her.

''Now you walk down the aisle together.''

The voice of the wedding coordinator yanked Sara back to reality.

What on earth was the matter with her? Had she lost her mind? She'd agreed to this charade in exchange for promised assistance in her quest. Losing herself in a game of make-believe wasn't part of that quest.

She was not Analise. This was not her wedding, the older man was not her father and Lucas was not her fiancé.

She pushed against Lucas's chest.

His heart pounding furiously, Lucas released Sara.

Around them the wedding party buzzed while the loudmouthed, pushy coordinator tried to get them quiet for another run-through or even two. They needed to have it down pat, she said, since it would be an entire week before the wedding, a lot of time to forget.

That was the last thing Lucas needed—to have to pretend to marry Sara again, to kiss her again.

Not that the kiss was a requisite part of the rehearsal. No, that had been entirely *his* idea. Actually, it hadn't even been his idea. His body, his lips had taken control, demanding to touch this woman who looked so much like his fiancée but affected him in a way Analise never had.

That was how he'd known for certain she wasn't Analise. Heaven help him, Analise had never set his hormones to boiling the way this woman did, and certainly never made him want to take care of her and protect her from the world.

Heck, the world needed protecting from Analise, he thought fondly. But Sara was a different story altogether. And he damn sure shouldn't be feeling this way about another woman a week before his wedding.

Nerves, he told himself. That's all it was. Because of

Analise's disappearance, he was hyped, his adrenaline pumping. He'd get away from here, do some deep breathing and get back to normal.

A tiny blond woman pushed through the crowd. "I can't believe my baby's getting married!" Clare Brewster exclaimed, reaching upward to embrace Sara.

Lucas held his breath. Did Sara look enough like Analise to fool her own mother? He needed to get her out of there fast…to protect her identity as well as to protect his out-of-kilter libido.

Sara leaned stiffly to accept Clare's embrace.

"Oh, good grief, Clare, don't start already," Analise's father admonished.

"Hush, Ralph. Go remove an appendix or lift a face or something. Do you feel all right, Analise? You look a little pale." She squinted upward, and Lucas repressed a smile at his future mother-in-law's vain reluctance to wear glasses. "You need some lipstick, sweetheart, and a little blusher. I'm not sure I like that new hairstyle. It makes you look so *old*, so grown-up. And where did you get that dress? Oh, I know, that look is trendy. It's just that it's so…so—"

Lucas placed a hand on Sara's shoulder. "Analise isn't feeling very good today. Why don't you all do another run-through of the wedding without us? We know our parts."

"You don't feel well, baby? What's the matter?"

"She's a little queasy, that's all. Prewedding jitters." Lucas wanted to bite his tongue as soon as he said it. Would anybody believe a mere wedding could make Analise jittery? "Or maybe a bug of some kind," he hastily added.

"We can't do this without the bride and groom," the coordinator protested.

"You certainly can," Clare said. "I'm taking my baby home. I'll have Annie make some of that potato soup you like, and you'll be all better by the rehearsal dinner tonight."

"No!" Sara and Lucas exclaimed in unison.

He'd forgotten about that stupid dinner and hadn't even considered the possibility that Clare might drag Sara home with her.

Ignoring them both, Clare clutched Sara's arm and tugged her toward the door.

Lucas flinched, expecting the worst. His future mother-in-law didn't know she was dragging off an ersatz daughter who was skilled in the art of self-defense.

When Sara merely gave him a panicked look over her shoulder rather than mauling Clare the way she'd done him, he sent up a short prayer of thanks.

He grabbed her other arm. "She needs to go with me," he said. He'd bargained with Sara for a couple of hours of her time, not an afternoon trapped by Analise's demanding parents who'd be sure to figure out immediately that Sara was not their headstrong daughter. For everybody's sake, he had to get her out of there. "We have some, uh, wedding arrangements to take care of."

"Nothing that can't wait," Clare argued. "My little girl's sick. She's coming home with me. You're not married to her yet." Clare was taking full advantage of her "daughter's" unaccustomed weakness.

"They're really important," Sara said in a strangled voice, "those arrangements Lucas and I need to take care of."

Clare patted Sara's cheek and smiled softly. "Can't it wait for one more day, sweetheart? Can't you be my little girl and let me take care of you one last time?"

A glazed expression came over Sara's face as she

looked down at Clare and, to Lucas's astonishment, she nodded slowly.

"Then I'm coming with her," he said. "After all, I'm a doctor." It was the best he could come up with on such short notice.

Clare frowned at him. "So is her father."

"And two doctors are better than one."

Right now he needed a doctor of a different sort, one to figure out why he'd ever thought this crazy idea would work in the first place. Unlike Analise, he wasn't given to doing impulsive things, and his first attempt was turning into a major disaster.

The three of them headed out of the church with Clare clucking and fussing over Sara's health.

Lucas caught a fleeting glimpse of Ralph's confused expression as Analise's father followed behind them. He knew something wasn't right with his daughter. Rather, the girl he thought was his daughter.

Somehow Lucas's attempt to keep the situation smooth had resulted in a sticky mess.

"Lucas, where's your car?" Clare asked as they exited the church.

"On Main Street," he answered truthfully. "It overheated."

"How did you get here?"

"I borrowed that car." He pointed to Sara's white sedan.

"Well, take it back and we'll see you at the house later."

"Analise has the keys."

"Give him the keys, baby."

Sara gave him another panic-stricken look as she handed him the car keys. He took them and Clare guided her into their Cadillac. Lucas gave her a smile he hoped was reassuring. "I'll be right behind you," he called.

Oh, boy, he thought as he trotted over to Sara's car.

Not only did he have to figure out some way to get Sara out of that house, but he'd forgotten about that damn dinner tonight.

He'd bridged a stream only to have a chasm open at his feet. He couldn't possibly ask Sara to pose as Analise again. All he'd done was delay the town's and her parents' knowledge of her defection. Ralph would be disappointed at Lucas's failure to bring stability to Analise's life. Clare would be a basket case. They were good people. He didn't want to see either of them upset.

And, since his acceptance in Briar Creek hinged on Ralph's acceptance of him, if Ralph's daughter rejected him, all the old talk would start again.

He pulled onto the street behind Ralph's car.

Maybe if he begged Sara...

Maybe if he let her attack him again, she'd feel guilty again and agree to this second favor.

In spite of the remembered pain, he had to smile at the way she'd defended herself. For someone so timid, she certainly knew her self-defense techniques and wasn't afraid to use them.

Sara Martin was an enigma, a tantalizing enigma, one he'd be tempted to explore if he weren't marrying Analise.

He frowned at his own thoughts.

He was engaged to Analise. He shouldn't be having thoughts like that about another woman. He never had before, and this was certainly no time to start.

So what if Analise and he didn't have that crazy, can't-live-without-each-other passion that the world insisted on writing songs about. He'd seen what that grand passion had done for his parents...ruined both their lives.

Analise was his friend, someone who would never make him lose control of his life or bring him pain. In spite of the fact that Analise was untamed and passionate, their relationship with each other was sane and safe.

Thank goodness he was marrying Analise and couldn't go chasing after tantalizing enigmas.

Chapter Three

Analise's house was every bit as intimidating as the church, Sara thought as they drove through the security gate and up the hill. Huge live oak, pecan and magnolia trees lined the entry and spread around the big, white Colonial structure. A smaller edifice would be hidden, but the Brewster house sat in regal splendor on top of the hill overlooking its domain. Bright roses twined in orderly fashion over trellises on each side of the front porch.

Lucas pulled in behind them and parked in the driveway in front of the large detached garage, then the four of them followed the sidewalk that wound to the front porch. Clare continued to talk, but Sara didn't hear anything she said. She looked down at the pebbled walk, at the velvety green lawn and called herself all kinds of an idiot. She'd always been so sedate, so sensible, so aware of the real world. She'd never indulged in daydreaming about things she couldn't have.

Until today.

She'd almost escaped until Analise's mother had reached up and touched her so gently and asked her to be her little girl one last time. She'd been determined she would get away from Analise's parents, from the church, from Lucas…but suddenly she'd slipped into that blasted fantasy again just the way she had while walking down the aisle. Without warning, an intense, aching loneliness had overwhelmed her, a longing to be cared for by a mother like Clare.

Her own mother—her adoptive mother—had loved her in her own way. June Martin had been a strict disciplinarian and she hadn't been a demonstrative person, but Sara could scarcely lament the lack of something she'd never had.

And she wasn't feeling that lack today, she assured herself. She was just getting caught up in the pretense, the way an actress sometimes got caught up in the role she was playing.

Which rationalization didn't help her situation. All she wanted to do right now was blurt out the truth and get away from these people, this house, this town. Go back to her dull little life and forget about finding her real mother who hadn't wanted her anyway so why was she so determined to find her?

Lucas's hand at the small of her back urged her up the steps of the porch and into the tiled entryway of the big house.

A crystal chandelier sparkled overhead and a wide, curving staircase loomed before her.

"Go on upstairs to your room, and I'll have Annie make you that soup," Clare instructed.

Lucas guided her toward the stairs. The enduring scents of old wood and lemon oil wrapped around her, speaking of a permanence she'd never known. She laid a tentative hand on the smooth, cool surface of the banister.

"Don't even think of sliding down that thing again," Ralph called.

She looked back to see him grinning at her, but his gaze was intent...assessing. He knew something was wrong.

She gave him a small smile. "Don't worry. I won't."

Lucas hustled her up the stairs and into Analise's room.

As soon as he closed the door behind them, she sank to the floor, drawing in huge gulps of air and expelling them in something between sobs and hysterical laughter. Lucas squatted beside her.

"I'm sorry, Sara. I thought this would be simple. I had no idea this was going to happen."

"What about the rehearsal dinner? You failed to mention that!"

Lucas ran his fingers through his hair, mussing his immaculate style. "I forgot. I was so upset about everything else, I forgot about that damn dinner. I don't suppose..."

"No! Absolutely not. This is making a nervous wreck out of me. I'm sorry. I just can't."

"That's okay. I shouldn't have asked. Look, if you can just eat some soup and then say you feel better, I'll get you out of here. That would be typical Analise behavior. She's always charging off somewhere, doing something bizarre. Like she did today."

"She goes off like that without telling her parents?" Sara asked incredulously. "I couldn't even go out in the yard without asking my mother."

"Analise always tells them, but it's usually after the fact, when it's too late for them to stop her. In this case, she told me, and I'm to tell her parents. She's kind of impulsive.''

''Sounds like it.'' *Flaky and irresponsible,* Sara would have said, though she found herself liking the absent Analise and wondering what it must be like to be so confident and so daring.

She leaned back against the door, pulled her knees to her chest and wrapped her arms around them. ''When I left Missouri, I was determined to change my life, but I didn't have quite this drastic a change in mind.''

''You're doing great,'' he assured her. ''You're to-tally safe as long as Clare doesn't put on her glasses...and she's so vain, I've never seen her wear them.''

''No, I'm not doing great. Her father suspects. Does she really slide down the banister?''

''That she does.'' He leaned back against the door beside her, one knee upraised with his hand resting on it. ''Analise is, um, high-spirited.''

''You must love her a lot.'' What a stupid thing to say, she chastised herself. He was marrying the woman. Of course he loved her.

''Love Analise? Well, sure. Yeah. We've been best friends since I moved back here to go into practice with her father six years ago.''

''He must be a very successful doctor.'' She looked around at all the opulence.

''He is,'' Lucas agreed. ''Successful and competent and a great guy. But this house belonged to Clare's family.''

And Lucas was marrying the impulsive daughter of this prominent family.

Sara got to her feet shakily and walked across the room. What on earth was she doing here? What made her think Analise Brewster would want to claim her as a sister, even if that far-fetched possibility should be true?

"This room is as big as some of the places where my mother and I lived."

"It used to be two rooms. Ralph and Clare had the wall knocked out when Analise was just a baby because she had too many toys for one room. Analise is an only child, and her parents overindulge her sometimes." He grinned. "Most times."

Sara stood for a moment studying the room with its plush white carpet, accented by colorful throw rugs. A red phone and a computer peeked from disorderly piles of paper on a rolltop desk. A white telephone—did Analise even have a private phone line?—sat on a nightstand next to a large bed with a white-eyelet spread almost hidden by bright throw pillows and stuffed animals. On one wall a large television stood guard over videotapes scattered casually around it. An elaborate stereo with compact discs in shining disarray occupied a corner, while an entire wall of built-in shelves was filled with books, photographs and assorted music boxes. In one corner, as if occupying a place of honor, a battered doll with remnants of red hair reclined in a doll carriage.

It was a comfortable room, one where Sara immediately and irrationally felt at home though she'd never lived in, or even visualized living in, such a room. Maybe it was the music boxes, something she'd have loved to collect if she'd had the money, or maybe—

"That doll looks a little like Analise," she said, more to herself than to Lucas.

"Not really. Analise is much taller and has more hair," Lucas teased.

Sara laughed. "I meant, she looks like a doll I used to have, a doll named Analise."

"Really? That's odd. I mean, it's an unusual name. What an odd coincidence that you named your doll Analise when you look so much like her."

"Yes, I guess it is." She picked up the doll and studied it curiously. "I have no idea where I heard the name. I saw that doll in the store and decided her name was Analise and I absolutely had to have her. Probably because she had red hair like me." *Or because she reminded me of a twin sister I remembered only on a subconscious level?* "We never had much money and we moved a lot, so I didn't get many toys. I understood and usually didn't complain, but this time I kept after my mother until she bought me that doll. Then I hung on to her until we moved to Iowa when I was nine. Somehow she got lost in that move, and I felt as though I'd lost my best friend."

She returned the doll to its carriage and smoothed its dress then turned back to Lucas.

He stood in front of the door like a sentinel, arms crossed over his chest, feet braced wide apart. "Seems pretty normal you'd feel that way if you moved around a lot. Making new friends is hard." He looked and sounded as if he knew from personal experience, and she recalled that he'd mentioned he'd moved *back* to town six years ago. But he didn't pursue the topic. Instead he inclined his head toward the shelves. "There's a picture of Analise—" he grinned "—the real one, not your doll."

Sara walked over and picked up the eight-by-ten color portrait. At first she was disappointed. From all the confusion of identity, she'd expected to feel as though she were looking into a mirror. "I can see a resemblance," she murmured, "but...I don't know. She's different. Prettier." However, the more she stared at the picture, the more she saw of herself—her eyes, her mouth, her nose.

Her sister?

Her twin sister?

Lucas came up behind her, his breath warm on her neck, and took it from her. "Resemblance, hell. She's not any prettier than you are. The same hairstyle, a little makeup, a big smile and it's you."

Sara moved a step away from Lucas's compelling nearness and picked up another picture, this one of Clare, Ralph and Analise, obviously taken a few years earlier. "Analise looks so happy."

"She is happy. Nothing's ever happened to make her sad."

The tone of Lucas's voice drew Sara's attention. She looked at him closely, beneath the polish, the perfect haircut and expensive clothes, to the pain tucked away at the very back of his eyes. She could see it as clearly as she saw his face. Maybe it wasn't that obvious to everyone, but she knew what to look for. To her chagrin, the added dimension made him even more attractive, tugged at her more surely than his hand on her arm in the church.

She had to get out of this house and away from these people before she lost complete control of her senses.

"Analise, why aren't you in bed?"

Sara whirled to see Clare standing in the doorway holding a tray with a bowl of steaming potato soup. In spite of everything, the smell made her mouth water and her soul relax. Her favorite comfort food as well as Analise's.

Another similarity.

Clare handed her tray to Lucas. "You can't wear that dress," she said as she crossed the room to the bed. "I don't suppose there's any chance you'll put on that nice robe your aunt Wilma sent you." She turned down the bed and plumped the pillows then looked at Sara. "Oh, well, it doesn't matter. Just go in the bathroom and change into something."

Sara spotted a door at one end of the room and bolted toward it. With any sort of luck, it would lead not to the bathroom but to another dimension.

The door revealed a huge walk-in closet crammed full of brightly colored clothes. Clare was going to think her daughter was really sick if she didn't even remember which door led to the bathroom.

Sara looked around desperately and finally spotted a pale pink quilted object that might be a robe dangling from a shelf in the back. She retrieved it, took a deep breath and returned to Lucas and Clare.

Clare smiled. "Why, thank you for humoring me, dear. Now I can tell your aunt Wilma you wore the robe."

Sara stole a glance at Lucas. He smiled, his eyes twinkling, and tilted his head toward a door at the other end of the room.

Analise's bathroom looked as though it had come straight out of the pages of a magazine. A huge gray marble Jacuzzi with shiny brass hardware dominated one side of the room with a matching vanity across the other. Someone had apparently cleaned this room as nothing but soft mauve towels and perfume bottles were in evidence.

A pale, frightened face stared back at Sara from the well-lighted mirror, a face that bore little resemblance to the vibrant, beautiful Analise in the picture Sara had

seen. For a fleeting moment, she thought how lucky
Analise was to have all these material things as well as
two loving parents and an attractive, caring fiancé
whose touch could create tantalizing tingles.

She shoved those thoughts aside. Envy never helped
anyone. Certainly not envy of someone else's fiancé.

She peeled off her clothes and put on the pink robe.
No wonder Analise didn't want to wear it. The fabric
was scratchy and much too warm for this time of the
year, plus the garment was large and bulky. But she
wouldn't have to wear it for long, just long enough to
eat some soup and get out of there.

As she turned to go, she saw hanging on the door a
brightly patterned silk robe of red swirled with green
and purple. She couldn't resist smiling. Even from what
little she knew of Analise, this robe seemed perfect for
her. She touched the soft fabric, letting it slide through
her fingers, and felt a curious connection with the missing Analise.

Lucas had promised that she could meet his fiancée
if she did this favor for him, and they'd gone way beyond "favor" at this point. However, she was no longer
sure she wanted to meet her look-alike. She was intimidated by everything to do with this woman she'd never
met, this woman who might be her sister.

She looked at herself again in the mirror. There were
differences, but she looked more like Analise than Analise looked like Clare and Ralph. Ralph had dark
brown, almost black, hair and hazel eyes, and Clare had
blond hair, blue eyes and a small, uptilted nose. No red
hair and green eyes or strong, straight nose.

Analise could very well be adopted, too.

Analise could very well be her twin.

Sara straightened her shoulders. Whatever the cost,

she had to meet Analise, had to know if they were related.

She left the bathroom, closing the door behind her, and went to sit on the bed.

"Omigosh!" She shot up, then reached behind her and pushed experimentally. "It's a water bed!"

"Analise, will you stop being silly and sit down," Clare demanded.

Sara lowered herself uneasily onto the unreliable surface, and Clare handed her the tray.

Sara took a tentative taste of the soup. "It's wonderful!"

"Good," Clare approved. "As soon as you finish eating, you take a nap. I'll come wake you in plenty of time to get ready for the rehearsal dinner."

"I'll stay with her for a while longer," Lucas said, coming to sit on the side of the bed.

Clare leaned over and brushed the wisps of hair back from Analise's face then kissed her forehead. Sara closed her eyes and tried not to enjoy the maternal gesture that belonged to Analise, not to her. But again, as at the wedding rehearsal, it was hard to keep in mind that this was all make-believe.

"Very well, Lucas," Clare said. "You can stay with her, but don't keep her awake."

The older woman bustled to the door, and Sara realized for the first time that Analise's parents seemed to have no problem with leaving her alone in her room with Lucas. Did that mean they knew and approved of Lucas and Analise...well, of their doing things married people did?

Lucas and Analise were engaged, and in this day and age, that sort of thing was accepted. There was no reason for her to feel that swift surge of...what? Pain? Envy?

Whatever it was, she refused to acknowledge or indulge it.

Clare paused at the door, looked back and sighed. "This will probably be the last time I get to take care of you," she said wistfully. "I don't suppose you want me to tuck Sara in with you this one last time?"

Sara's fingers clutched the tray in her lap convulsively. She heard Lucas gasp. What on earth was Analise's mother saying?

"Oh, don't give me that look. I know you're all grown-up and too old for dolls, but I saw you cuddling Sara and talking to her just last week. Lucas, don't you dare make fun of Analise. Of course she'll want to take that old doll with her when you get married. She's an only child, and that doll's been her pretend sister since she was just a little thing."

Chapter Four

The door closed behind Clare, and Lucas turned to Sara. Her gaze was still riveted on the door and she looked as confused as he felt.

"What's going on here?" he asked. "Who are you? Why does Analise have a doll with your name and you have a doll with her name?"

She shook her head slowly. As if in a daze, she stood and set the lap tray on the nightstand. Managing somehow to look graceful and regal even in that ridiculous robe, she crossed the room and picked up Analise's picture again.

"Is Analise adopted?" she asked.

"No, of course not. Well, I don't think so." He shifted from one foot to the other. "I don't know," he admitted. "It's never come up."

"She doesn't look like either Clare or Ralph."

"I hadn't thought about it, but you're right. She doesn't."

Sara set the picture back on the shelf and shifted her

gaze to him, her eyes alight with sudden hope. "I need to find out if it's possible she's my twin."

"Your twin?" He scowled. From the time this woman had kneed him in the groin, crushed his shin and held him at bay with pepper spray, this situation had become more and more bizarre. "Analise is an only child. She doesn't have any sisters, certainly not a twin."

Sara darted back to sit beside him, her cheeks flushed with becoming color, and he could feel the charge of energy surrounding her. "But what if she's not an only child? What if she was adopted? What if she has a twin sister?"

Sara's animation made her more delectable than ever. He wanted to agree with her just to please her, to let her maintain that glow. But he couldn't. She was getting a little far-out.

"Are you saying your mother might have had twins and given up your sister for adoption? Sara, you're not making sense."

"Yes, I am. I was adopted." Her voice softened, sadness spreading a cloud over her enthusiasm. "I just found out a year ago when my mother had kidney failure and I offered to donate a kidney. The tests showed I couldn't be her daughter, and she finally admitted the truth to me. So maybe I had a twin sister, and we were both adopted."

Adopted. That explained a few things, like her response to Clare's kindness and her need to prove Analise was her sister. With the only mother she'd ever known dead and not her biological mother after all, Sara must feel very alone in the world. She was probably desperate to find a family. Nevertheless, he had to shatter her ill-founded hopes about Analise. "Twins adopted by different people? That's impossible."

"Why is it impossible? Analise and I look so much alike her own mother couldn't tell the difference. And look at the other evidence. Even twins separated at birth always seem to have some sort of a connection. I studied about it in school. They wear the same kind of clothes, marry people with the same names, go into the same professions."

"But you and Analise dress completely differently." This whole thing was so crazy, he didn't dare tell Sara that Analise, unable to find employment in her chosen field in Briar Creek and forbidden by her parents to move to a larger city, did volunteer work at the library.

"We do dress differently, that's true. But she wanted to be an entomologist, and so did I. I studied library science only because my mother insisted." She rose and moved around the room again. "How do you explain the coincidence of the dolls? And look at all the music boxes Analise has." She picked up one he'd given Analise for her birthday a couple of years ago, a crystal unicorn on a base of mirrors. Carefully she turned it over, wound the key and listened to the strains of "Born Free" as they tinkled into the room.

"What about the music boxes?" he asked.

"I've always loved them. Every time we'd go into a store, I'd search for the music boxes, then I'd choose one and wind it up and listen until my mother found me." She looked at him, her chin tilted defiantly. "I've lived my whole life with lies. Now I'm going to find the truth."

"In Briar Creek? Why here? Did your mother tell you that your birth mother came from here?"

The tilt to her chin drooped slightly, and Lucas felt

a momentary pang that he'd been the one to dampen her enthusiasm.

"Not exactly," she said. "After she died, I found a crumpled pay stub that had fallen through a hole in the pocket of her coat and lodged in the lining. The coat had been cleaned several times and only the name of the bank survived. The First National Bank of Briar Creek, Texas. That's why I came here. It's the only clue I have."

Lucas flinched at the mention of the bank where his father had worked, the bank that had sent his father to prison, but Sara's expression was guileless.

"That bank was bought out several years ago," he said, watching her closely for any reaction.

"I know. I tried to call them. I found out some big banking company from Dallas took them over, and they wouldn't tell me anything. So I had to come here. It's a small town. Surely someone here knew my mother. My adoptive mother. Maybe somebody will even know who my real mother is."

"What about your father? The one who raised you, I mean. Your mother's husband. You haven't mentioned him. Where is he? What does he think about all this?"

She held the music box up to the sunshine coming through the windows and watched the play of rainbow colors as the light refracted through the crystal onto the mirrored surface. "I don't have a father," she said, the words matter-of-fact, detached, though he suspected the feelings associated with her statement weren't nearly so unemotional. "My mother never married. She always told me he deserted us when he found out she was pregnant with me. But, of course, that part wasn't true."

He rose slowly and crossed the room to her. Cupping her face in his hands, he forced her to look at him.

"Sara, you're a beautiful young woman with your life ahead of you. Forget the past. It doesn't matter. All that matters is what you do from now on."

"What would you do if you didn't know who your parents were, what they looked like, what kind of lives they'd led, whether you had brothers and sisters, if your father was a rocket scientist or in prison?"

Lucas dropped his hands. "What if you do find out he's in prison?"

She winced at the harshness in his voice, turned away and busied herself with repositioning the music box on the shelf.

"Maybe you're better off not knowing," he said softly. "Having a family isn't always what it's cracked up to be."

"Neither is ignorance," she said firmly.

Lucas smiled. "Touché. Okay, Sara Martin from Deauxville, Missouri. I'll give you credit for another likeness to Analise. You're both stubborn. So, what can I do to help? That was our agreement. You help me, and I'll help you."

He looked into her eyes which were the color of the magnolia leaves outside the window. That was strange. They were the same shade of green as Analise's, but he'd never thought of Analise's eyes as being like the magnolia leaves. Maybe it was because the scent of magnolias seemed to surround Sara, soft and sweet with an underlying, tangy hint of lemon. Her skin reminded him of magnolia flowers—creamy and velvety and fragile.

Helping Sara, spending any more time around her, might not be such a good idea. He enjoyed it entirely too much for an engaged man.

"Thanks, but other than introducing me to Analise when she returns, I can manage on my own."

Good. That let him off the hook.

"Absolutely not," he heard someone say. "A deal's a deal." He had to be the one who'd said it. He was the only person in the room with his lips moving.

What the heck. He might as well deal with and get over this strange fascination he had for Sara. If by some fluke she did prove to be a distant relative of Analise, he could be seeing her every Christmas, Thanksgiving and birthday. Drooling over the in-law would most certainly not come under the heading of proper etiquette.

"You can do one thing for me," she said firmly. "Tell me where Analise gets her hair cut."

"What...? Why do you want to know that?"

"So I can get my hair cut like hers and see how much I really look like her."

"You can't do that!"

"Why not?"

Good question. Because he was enthralled with the luxurious length of her hair? Because he liked her just the way she was?

"Because it's Saturday, and you'll never be able to get an appointment. They're always booked solid on Saturdays."

She frowned, picked up the picture of Analise and looked at it again. "Then I'll cut it myself."

"You can't do that!"

Taking the picture with her, she marched into the bathroom and began yanking open drawers.

He followed her in. "What are you looking for?"

"Scissors."

"This is crazy!"

She pulled out a large, shiny pair. "Please, Lucas.

You don't understand how important this is to me. I
never had any family except my mother...no father, no
brothers or sisters, no grandparents, no aunts and uncles.
Not even any close girlfriends because we moved so
often. And then I discovered I didn't really have my
mother.''

Lucas leaned back against the marble vanity and
folded his arms. "No, I guess I don't understand. Having relatives doesn't necessarily mean you have a family.''

"What happened to your family, Lucas?" she asked,
her gentle words probing, touching something hidden
safely away deep inside, making him want to talk to
her, to spill his guts.

"Oh, hell," he said instead, slid out Analise's
makeup stool and took the scissors from Sara. "Sit
down. You want your hair cut, I'll cut it for you. It
can't be any harder than removing an appendix."
Maybe if she looked exactly like Analise, he could get
rid of these disturbing feelings, could view her with the
same affectionate tolerance he had for Analise.

She sat obediently, hands folded in her lap. He pulled
the long braid from the bulky robe and loosened the
strands, the way he'd done on the street, only this time
he steeled himself not to get lost in the silky depths, not
to notice the warmth from her body that lingered in her
hair or the scent of magnolia blossoms that wafted up
to him.

"Are you sure you want to do this?" he asked, the
words coming out oddly husky. Her hair spread across
the ghastly pink robe like a thick, burnished veil, lying
in uneven waves left from the braiding. Not trendy or
stylish but, oh, so tantalizing.

"Lucas?''

"What?"

"I said I'm sure. Go ahead."

He lifted a section of hair and drew a comb through it. He'd often watched in the mirror as his mother cut his. He knew Analise's was all one length except for her bangs. This couldn't be so tough.

He let the silky strands slide from his fingers then shook his head and laid the scissors on the vanity.

To his surprise, Sara spun around on the stool, retrieved the scissors and whacked a large chunk out of her hair. "There. Now you have to finish it or I'll look really strange." She hesitated then added quietly, "At the dinner tonight."

"You don't have to go to the dinner tonight. That wasn't part of our original deal."

"But I will go if you want me to so you won't have to explain where Analise is. If we fix my hair and makeup like hers, we can do it."

Sara wasn't sure why she was suddenly offering to go to the rehearsal dinner with Lucas. She'd made the offer with the idea of bribing him to cut her hair for her, to help her look like Analise, but that wasn't all of it. She was reluctant to lose contact, however briefly, with Lucas. He was, after all, the one link she had to this person who might be her sister.

Lucas moved closer to her, his large, surprisingly gentle hands again lifting her hair, making her scalp tingle, sending delightful sensations through her entire body. In the interest of being brutally honest with herself, she had to question whether her reluctance to lose contact with Lucas was entirely due to his link to Analise. She enjoyed being with him, being touched by him, far more than was safe or sensible.

She sat rigid while he carefully snipped off her hair.

This fascination with Lucas was not good. Even if he weren't Analise's fiancé, he came from a totally different world than Sara's. He was a doctor, an associate of the town's founding family. How often had her mother told her that such men had no place in their lives for people like her?

Not that she still believed everything her mother had drummed into her, but twenty-five years of training was difficult to throw off. And she did feel uncomfortable in Analise and Lucas's world.

"There," he said, laying the scissors on the vanity and stepping back. "I only have two things to say about this deal. Operating on people is a lot easier than cutting hair, and I sure hope curling will hide the mistakes."

Sara looked at herself in the mirror. Feathery bangs spiked her forehead, and her hair stopped just past her shoulders. Experimentally she tossed her head. The hair swished around her face and neck. "It feels so light."

Lucas stood behind her, his expression intense. Their gaze met in the mirror.

"What do you think?" she asked.

He didn't say anything for a long moment, and she was astonished to realize how much she wanted his approval.

"I think you look like Analise." He shrugged. "Or she looks like you." Finally he smiled. "You're on your own with the makeup, though."

He helped her find hot rollers and makeup, then, contrary to his assertion, guided her through the process of becoming his fiancée.

A few minutes later she saw Analise staring back at her from the mirror.

Well, not quite Analise. The face in the mirror still

looked uncertain and tentative rather than animated and eager for the next adventure.

"Unbelievable," Lucas murmured. "You're so much like her and so unlike her."

He'd noticed it, too.

She bit her lip. "Before we go to that dinner, I need to return to my room at the Sleep Well Motel and change to another dress. Nobody seemed to like the one I had on today. Obviously it wasn't the kind Analise would wear."

"Wear one of Analise's."

She spun around on the stool to face him. "I couldn't do that!"

"Sure you could. You may be a little bit slimmer, but you're pretty much the same size."

"That's not what I mean! I can't wear somebody else's clothes without asking. It's bad enough I've used her makeup and curlers."

"Analise won't mind. She's always loaning out or even giving away her possessions."

"She sounds like a very generous person." *And you, Sara Martin, are not at all generous to resent Lucas's fiancée having so many wonderful traits, so many traits obviously pleasing to him.*

Lucas shrugged. "*Things* don't mean much to Analise. She's always had plenty of money to replace them. If she were here, she'd loan you a dress or two. Heck, she'd give them to you. Let's go check out her closet." He gestured across the room and grinned. "You know, the first bathroom."

"You haven't, have you?"

"Haven't what?"

"Always had plenty of money."

He hesitated before answering, looking away from

her. "No, I haven't. I was the half-Indian kid from the wrong side of town. We moved away when I was four because my father...because my family wasn't welcome here. I went to medical school on scholarships, most of them funded by Ralph Brewster, then he took me into his medical practice. I owe everything to him. He gave me a chance when nobody else would. That's why I don't want to see him or Clare hurt and I do want to prove to him and to everybody else around here that I can be trusted." He gave her a crooked grin. "And that includes getting my fiancée to her own wedding rehearsal."

She wanted to ask him more, wanted to ask why his family hadn't been welcome in Briar Creek, if that had anything to do with the pain that lived at the back of his eyes. But he'd glossed over that part of his life, skipping straight to medical school. And it was none of her business anyway.

"Don't worry," she assured him. "We're halfway there. One event down and one to go."

Suddenly she wanted to help him for more than selfish reasons, even more than not wanting to see Clare's kind face distorted in pain. She knew only too well how it felt to be unwelcome in a community. In fact, she had no idea how it felt to be welcome. She crossed the room to the big walk-in closet she'd accidentally blundered into earlier.

Lucas followed and shoved aside several articles of clothing to pull out a vibrant turquoise dress. "This should look great with your hair."

She touched the fabric. Silky, just like the colorful robe. She'd never had anything so soft against her skin, and she couldn't help wondering how it would feel. As sensual as Lucas's lips had felt on hers at the rehearsal?

She took a step back, away from the garment and from Lucas. The dress, like Lucas, belonged to Analise. She had no right to enjoy either of them. "It's...short. Is Analise shorter than I am?"

"No, I'd say you're about the same height. It's supposed to be this length." Though the closet had a light, the room was dim after the sun-bright space of the bedroom, and Lucas's dark eyes seemed to burn with inner fires. She was entirely too aware of his presence directly behind her in the confines of the closet that suddenly seemed to have become much smaller.

"Okay." She snatched the dress and darted out of the closet.

Back in the bathroom, she pulled off the bulky robe and slipped into the dress Lucas had chosen. The fabric slid over her bare skin like the smooth, scented water of a bubble bath.

The fit was perfect, but she'd been right about the length. It stopped a couple of inches above her knees.

She'd never worn anything that showed her knees, but she knew that other women did, that this length was stylish.

Feeling self-conscious and exposed, she opened the door and stepped back into the room.

Lucas blinked. "Wow," he said softly, his gaze gliding over her from head to toe. "You look—" He cleared his throat. "Nice. Good fit. Now shoes. I don't suppose there's any chance you could wear Analise's shoes, too. That would be too much of a coincidence."

Sara glanced back into the bathroom, at her comfortable loafers. "No, I wear an unusual size. I have my good shoes at the motel room."

"I can pick them up when I go home to change."

Panic seized Sara at Lucas's words. "You're going

to leave me? Alone? What do I do if Clare or Ralph comes back?"

He walked over to her, tucked one finger under her chin and smiled. "Do the exact opposite of whatever first comes to mind. If you feel like crying, laugh instead. If you feel frightened, act brave. Anything you can think of that's absolutely outrageous, do it. Don't let Clare push you around. If she tells you to do something you don't want to do, tell her no. Clare's kind of bossy and demanding, but Analise always does as she pleases. Hey, anybody with the guts to let me cut her hair has got the guts to carry this off."

Do the exact opposite of whatever first comes to mind. She was completely unlike Analise. The similarity in appearance must be a coincidence, not evidence of a close relationship. "I'll do my best," she said. "Don't stay gone very long."

"I won't." He stepped back and looked down at her feet. "What size shoe do you wear?"

"Nine narrow. I don't go into a shoe store and ask to see certain shoes. I just ask what they have in my size."

His throat muscles contracted and released as he swallowed. "So does Analise. Wear a nine narrow, I mean."

They stared at each other in silence for a moment, then he went back to the closet and returned with a pair of multicolored slippers.

She pulled the chair away from Analise's desk and sat in it. Rather than handing her the shoes, Lucas knelt and slid the first shoe onto her foot. For a fleeting moment, Sara felt like Cinderella, her foot an exact fit for the glass slipper, preparing to go to the ball with the prince.

But she wasn't.

She was plain Sara Martin, dressed in Analise Brewster's clothes, preparing to go to the rehearsal dinner with Analise's fiancé.

"This is getting kind of creepy," Lucas said, his fingers warm on her ankle. "I don't suppose you've got a heart-shaped birthmark on your left thigh?"

Sara eased her foot out of Lucas's grasp as his words reminded her of the intimate relationship he had with her look-alike. "No. Does Analise?"

He rose slowly, his gaze holding hers. "I have no idea. I was making a joke. Not a very good one, I guess." He cleared his throat and brushed invisible lint from his pants. "I'll go home and change then come back and take you to the rehearsal dinner. Do you need anything from your motel room now that we have the shoe question settled?"

"No. Nothing." Her common sense, but she'd apparently left that all the way back in Deauxville.

He paused at the door. "Just remember, be brave, be outrageous and don't take any guff from Clare."

Sara nodded, though she wasn't at all sure she could follow those directions.

Lucas stepped outside Analise's room and closed the door behind him. He hated to leave Sara. She was so dependent on him.

On the other hand, he needed to get away from her for a while and get his head back on straight.

He was engaged to a beautiful woman, a woman he adored. Well, at least he liked her a lot, and she liked him. Maybe they weren't wildly, passionately in love, but that was good. He'd never had any desire for that kind of insanity, for having his entire life disrupted. His marriage to Analise would make Ralph Brewster very happy, and he owed Ralph, big time, not to mention how much he genuinely liked both Ralph and Clare.

This was no time to let a pair of magnolia-leaf eyes or magnolia-blossom skin make him forget all that.

He marched downstairs, planting each foot firmly on the next step. He was in control here.

"Are you leaving, Lucas?" Clare asked as she emerged from the library.

"Going home to change clothes, then I'll be back."

"You don't need to return. We could just meet you at the restaurant. It would give me a few more minutes with my daughter."

Lucas chuckled. "Clare, you act like you're never going to see Analise again. I only live two miles from here. She'll probably spend more time at home after we get married than she did before."

The phone rang.

She smiled up at him. "I know, I know. All right, we'll see you in a little while." She reached for the extension on the hall table. "Hello?"

Lucas moved from the last step onto the floor.

"Analise?" Clare spoke into the telephone, obviously puzzled.

Chapter Five

Lucas spun around and snatched the phone away from Clare. "Analise! You caught me just as I was going out the door." He covered the mouthpiece. "Isn't that just like Analise? Calling from upstairs instead of walking down."

"Lucas? What are you talking about? I'm not calling from upstairs. I'm calling from the airport in Rattlesnake Corners, Wyoming, and I'm on the first floor. Did you get my note?"

"Yes, sure did." He gave Clare what he hoped was a reassuring smile.

"So did you get the rehearsal rescheduled?"

"Don't worry about a thing. I've got it all under control."

"I knew you would! You're so capable! I don't know what I'd do without you! Maybe you could reschedule our wedding, too."

"What?" Lucas could feel the perspiration beading on his forehead as panic shoved its sharp edge between his ribs and into his chest. "That's not a possibility," he said firmly. With almost a thousand invitations already out? What on earth was Analise thinking?

"Okay, if it comes to that, we'll worry about it later."

"If it comes to that?" Lucas tried unsuccessfully to control the panic that crept into his voice. "What are you talking about?"

"Oh, relax! You're going to be so excited when I tell you what I'm doing here! I'm going to have such a surprise for you!"

Lucas had a feeling *distressed* or *upset* or even *horror-stricken* would more accurately describe the way he was going to be than *excited*…the way he was rapidly becoming, in fact. From the corner of his eye he could see Clare's pleasant features wrinkling into a worried frown. "That's a great idea," he babbled into the phone, drawing a shaky hand across his damp upper lip. "Wear whatever you want. When do you think you'll be coming downstairs?" He accented the last question, hoping she'd give him a clue as to when she planned to return.

"Lucas, you're not making any sense. How can I come downstairs? I told you, I'm on the first floor now. Have you been sampling the champagne already?" She laughed gaily, completely unconcerned with the havoc she was causing. "Oh, I've got to go! That might be Nick coming in the door now! Tell Mom and Dad I'm fine and I'll be home in a few days!"

Nick?

The line went dead.

"Uh, um, goodbye, Analise. See you in a couple of, uh, hours!" He hung up the phone, looked at Clare and shrugged, trying to smile as though everything was normal. "Your impulsive daughter."

Clare took a step toward the stairs. "I'd better go up and check on her, see if she feels any better. Maybe she's worse, so sick she couldn't come to the door but had to telephone down."

Lucas laid a restraining hand on her arm. "No, that's not a good idea. She, uh, she said she was going to take a nap. She's probably asleep already."

Clare cast a concerned glance up the stairs.

"Clare, your daughter's fine." Analise had just told him she was. However, he wasn't so sure about the woman in Analise's room. "You worry too much."

Clare wrung her hands. "I know. It's just that…she's the only daughter I have." She lifted a beseeching gaze to Lucas. "I'm so glad you two are getting married. I can count on you to take good care of her."

Unlike the man Analise had been involved with in college. Clare didn't speak the words, but they hung in the air nevertheless.

He took Clare's hands between both of his. "I'll do my best. I swear I will take care of her." But his *best* when pitted against Analise's *worst* seemed a little weak right now. "Analise is, um, headstrong." That was kind of like saying Texas in July was warm.

"Yes, she is. Ralph and I are to blame. We've spoiled her outrageously, and I don't regret one moment of it. I wish…" Her blue eyes misted and seemed to focus somewhere beyond Lucas, beyond the present.

"You wish you'd had more children, that Analise had a sister," he said, putting into words something he'd heard Ralph and Clare discuss in vague terms over the years, though never in Analise's presence. He'd never asked why they'd been unable to have another child or why they hadn't adopted one. Now Sara's assertion that she and possibly Analise were adopted came back to him. Had Clare and Ralph been unable to have children at all? Was Analise adopted?

Clare focused on him again, blinked away the hint of moisture and smiled. "We're gaining a son. If Analise hadn't agreed to marry you, we'd have had to adopt you. And now we're counting on you and Analise to fill this big old house with lots of grandchildren."

Lucas leaned over and kissed Clare's carefully made-up cheek. "I'll do my best," he promised.

Though the thought of making grandchildren with Analise seemed almost incestuous. How was it possible he could love Analise like a sister yet feel decidedly unbrotherly lust for the woman upstairs who looked exactly like her? The only kisses he and Analise had shared had been as chaste as the one he'd just planted on Clare's cheek. He'd thought marriage would change that. Now he wasn't so sure.

He turned to go but stopped at the door.

He couldn't leave Sara trapped in Analise's room for two hours. Clare was bound to go up and check on her, and Sara was so helpless, so vulnerable. She'd be bound to crack, and then both Clare and Sara would be hurt. He couldn't allow that to happen to either of them.

"I just thought of something I need to talk to Analise about." He whirled around and charged up the stairs, taking them two at a time.

"But you said she was napping," Clare called after him.

He ignored Clare as well as the warning bell that clanged somewhere in the back of his mind, demanding to know why he was so eager to get back to Sara, so determined to rescue her.

* * *

Sara tensed when she heard footsteps pounding up the stairs. Carefully she set down the family picture of Analise, Clare and Ralph that she'd been studying and braced herself for the invasion of, judging from the heavy sounds, Analise's father. He'd probably figured out she was an impostor and was going to send her packing. She astonished herself with the despair that possibility brought, with the depth of her desire to revel in this fantasy world for a little while longer.

Maybe if she slid down the banister, Ralph would be convinced.

And maybe she'd have a cracked skull.

She clenched her fists against her chest, the tension physically painful, as the door flew open.

Lucas burst into the room and she let out her breath in a relieved gasp.

He paused just inside and gave her a smile she would have described as *goofy* if it had been anywhere other than on Lucas's sophisticated features.

Impulsively she started toward him then drew herself up short. He might be the only person who knew who she was and he might be smiling at her, but he was still a relative stranger, not someone she could run to for support.

"I see you're up and dressed," he said loudly, tilting his head toward the open doorway. "Are you feeling better?"

"I feel fine." Then, realizing that he was speaking for the benefit of whoever was listening downstairs, she repeated more loudly, "I feel fine."

"We still have those last-minute details to go over if you're up to it."

"I am. I'm all better."

And eager to go with Lucas, to escape from Analise's room and the possibility of exposure as a fraud.

Or just eager to go with Lucas? a small voice taunted.

To escape from Analise's room and the possibility of discovery, she repeated firmly.

"Let's go, then."

With a sense of relief at leaving the strange room and a sense of loss at leaving the room that almost felt familiar, Sara went downstairs with Lucas.

Clare looked up anxiously as they approached. "Are you sure you're up to this?"

"I'm fine," Sara assured her.

Clare lifted a cool hand to Sara's cheek. "You look a little flushed."

The motherly gesture was so touching, it almost brought tears to her eyes. Impulsively Sara laid her hand over Clare's and smiled. "The soup was wonderful. I'm all better. Just nerves, I guess."

That was certainly true. Between the deception and Lucas's nearness, she was surprised Clare only found her *a little flushed.* She felt as if her entire body and soul were on fire.

Clare stood in the doorway and waved as she and Lucas drove away. Analise was a lucky woman, Sara thought as she returned the wave.

"First," Lucas said, "we need to see about getting my car towed to a garage, then we'll figure out how to go about finding your parents."

She looked at Lucas's strong profile, at his long fingers wrapped around the steering wheel of her clunker car.

Analise was a very lucky woman.

* * *

Lucas's red brick ranch-style home on a pleasantly shady residential street was not as intimidating as Analise's mansion. In fact, this was the most comfortable Sara had felt all afternoon.

She accepted a glass of iced tea from Lucas and forced herself to lean back on the soft, cool leather of the sand-colored sofa. The large, high-ceilinged living room was done in earth tones, and the paintings on the off-white walls were landscapes of trees and forests. Eucalyptus branches in a couple of dried-plant arrangements combined with the leather to give the room a clean, woodsy fragrance. It lacked the opulence of the Brewsters' home, and also the warmth. Though everything was perfect, she suspected he'd had it done by an interior decorator. It didn't reflect the depths she'd seen in Lucas.

Nevertheless, she was able to take a deep breath and relax for the moment.

The irony of that thought hit her as she watched Lucas take a seat in the large recliner that coordinated with the sofa, though its color was a couple of shades lighter. A few weeks ago, instead of being more relaxed, she would have been terrified at the thought of being in a man's home alone with him.

And not just a man, but a man with money, even if he was not quite so blatantly moneyed as the Brewsters.

But today she'd learned that being terrified was a relative condition. Walking into that church and posing as Analise had been terrifying. Watching Lucas walk out the door of Analise's room the first time without her had been terrifying. In comparison, her present situation was relaxing.

Well, almost.

The feelings Lucas created in her, while certainly enjoyable, were the opposite of relaxing.

He lifted his glass and took a long drink of his iced tea, the muscles in his throat moving as he swallowed. His day had been, she realized, as stressful as hers.

"Do you live here alone?" she asked, then bit her lip. Had that sounded as though it came from the mouth of a naive, small-town girl? "I mean, this isn't your family home where you live with your parents, like Analise does with hers, is it?"

"No sign of a woman's touch, you mean? You're right. This isn't my family home. We—" He scowled into his glass of tea, then looked up again, his expression urbane and veiled. "Like I said, we moved away when I was four. I came back but my folks didn't."

"Where do they live?" She asked the question though she had a feeling he wouldn't want to answer it.

"They're in Pennsylvania now."

"Pennsylvania? That's a long way from here. This town must have made a really strong impression on you that you'd come such a long distance to a place you left when you were four."

He gazed at her silently for several seconds, and she thought he was going to ignore her implied question. "Yes," he finally said. "It's a long way. But we lived within a couple of hours of Briar Creek for ten years before we moved."

"Is that why your parents weren't here for the rehearsal? That it's such a long trip and they couldn't stay for the entire week?" It was possible they had been there and she hadn't known it, but somehow she didn't think so.

"Yeah, that's why."

"But they are coming for your wedding?"

For just a moment the curtain lifted from Lucas's eyes, and Sara saw a heartbreaking mixture of pain, longing and fear. "I don't know. They're invited, but...I don't know." He cleared his throat and shifted in his chair. "So, tell me everything you can about your mother, adoptive or biological. We can't do much until Monday, but we might as well try to figure out where we need to start."

Hope bubbled through Sara even as she noted that Lucas had changed the subject from his family to hers. Her mother would have said it was because he didn't deem it proper to talk to her, a nobody, about his life. But she didn't think that was it. She had a feeling Lucas would be just as reluctant to discuss his background with anyone. Something in his veiled expression as he'd looked up from his tea, in the very air around him, whispered of secrets Lucas would just as soon keep buried.

And now Sara didn't want to tell him about her own tawdry past.

Which was absurd. What difference did it make what Lucas Daniels thought about her?

She took a deep breath and straightened her shoulders. Lucas was offering to help her find her biological heritage. In order to do that, he'd need all the meager store of data she could provide.

"My mother's name was June Martin. As I said, she always told me that my father had deserted her when he found out she was pregnant with me. Then when she was sick and the doctor told me I wasn't her daughter, she admitted I was adopted. But all she'd tell me was that my mother had been very poor, and my father, a wealthy man, had refused to marry her because his parents didn't approve of her, so she gave up her baby. Me.''

"And the only clue you have that she came from Briar Creek is the pay stub in her coat lining.''

Sara nodded. "We moved a lot. We only kept the essentials.''

"Do you have a copy of your birth certificate?''

"Yes, I found it after my mother died. I have it back at the motel, but it's not going to be of much use. It's a fake.''

Lucas lifted a dark eyebrow.

"Good enough to get me into school, but not good enough to fool the court clerk. It was supposed to be from Los Angeles, but when I sent a copy out there, the clerk wrote back and said it was a fake.''

"Did you live in Los Angeles at one time?''

"Not that I know of. My mother never mentioned it. Of course—'' she grinned wryly ''—there were a lot of things my mother never mentioned. It's possible I was born there, though the hospital named on my birth certificate never existed. Albert Martin, the man listed as my father, is a common name, but none of the Albert Martins I found in the area fit the criteria for my father, so that's probably phony, too. In fact, I'm not even sure my mother legally adopted me. As a single woman, in those days she'd have been considered low on the list of adoptive parents.''

"It doesn't sound like she did it legally. Adoptions come with a new birth certificate. A real one.''

Sara looked down at her hands. Dry and a little rough from handling paper all day at work then going home to wash dishes, they clutched the glass of amber tea that matched the glass Lucas held and probably another six or ten or more in the kitchen cabinet. With the breakage of moving so much, she and her mother rarely had even two glasses or plates that matched.

She had no parents, no family name, no home. She didn't even have a real birth certificate.

Suddenly she felt as much out of place here as she had in the church or in the Brewsters' house. But if living with June Martin had taught her nothing else, she had at least learned to hide her feelings.

She lifted her chin and forced herself to speak clearly and without any distress in her voice. "That's not the only reason I have for thinking my adoption wasn't legal. We lived our entire lives in hiding, running from one small town to another. I remember living in Nebraska, Minnesota, Iowa, Illinois and Missouri, and I'm pretty sure we were in South Dakota and Wyoming before that."

"Wyoming?"

"I was only four or five when we moved, but I kind of remember it. Why? Is that significant?"

He shrugged. "Not really. That's where Analise is. Just a coincidence."

Her gaze locked with his. *Another coincidence.* Though the words weren't spoken, they hung in the air between them, teasing and tantalizing, their meaning just out of reach.

"Well," Sara continued, "anyway, we lived in all those different places. And my mother was very strict that we couldn't make friends, we couldn't let anybody know anything about us. She was obsessed with the idea that somebody might try to kidnap me. She used to drill me daily on her list of rules. 'What do you do if a stranger comes up to you?' 'Run.' 'What do you do if a stranger asks your name?' 'Don't tell him anything.' When I started school, I was so paranoid. I was afraid to answer roll call and admit who I was. I got counted absent the first six weeks until the teacher noticed she had class work from a student who showed up on the rolls as not being there.''

Lucas's eyes widened, and she smiled, giving him permission to be amused at her nontraditional past.

He laughed, then shook his head in amazement. ''Are you making that up?''

''No! I was an adult before I could see the humor, but it's all true. She drilled me daily, and then when I was twelve, she and I took self-defense classes, and after that, we practiced the techniques regularly.''

Lucas's smile flinched as his hand slid along his thigh, stopping just short of protecting the area she'd assaulted earlier. ''You learned well. I have to admit, I was relieved that you didn't toss Clare over your shoulder when she started dragging you home with her from the church.''

Sara laughed softly. ''If my mother were here, she'd tell me that you, Clare and Ralph are all part of some plot to kidnap me.''

Lucas shook his head slowly. ''She really was paranoid.''

''Very. And I grew up believing her. I was a teenager before I figured out she was a little off in her thinking.''

''Brainwashing.''

''What?''

''It's a form of brainwashing. Your mother kept you isolated, kept you from any influence but her, and fed you her beliefs. Of course you bought into them. I think it's a miracle you were able to discard them as early as your teenage years. You're a strong lady, Sara Martin.''

Sara could feel her face flush hotly at the compliment, even if it wasn't the kind men usually gave to women. She looked down at the glass of tea she still held. The ice was melting and the outside was beaded with condensation. Hurriedly, before it could drip onto Analise's dress, she set the glass on a coaster on the polished wood surface of the large square coffee table.

"So," she said briskly, "putting the phony birth certificate together with my mother's paranoia, I'm assuming my real mother gave me away, literally. Handed me over. And my mother always worried that she'd come to take me back."

Lucas nodded slowly. "It's possible you were born in Los Angeles, but it's just as likely that your mother might have chosen that city for your birth certificate because it's so big it would be hard to find information or disprove information. Especially since this would have all taken place before information was computerized. It's just as likely you could have been born here."

"Or anywhere. I know I don't have a lot to go on." Hearing herself put into words for the first time how little she actually knew, Sara felt an insidious hopelessness creep over her. For so long she'd told herself the information she had was enough because it had to be. The alternative was unthinkable—to continue to live this half life of no roots, no identity.

Suddenly she was hit with the realization that it might not be enough, that just needing something desperately didn't necessarily make it happen.

"My best man's a lawyer," Lucas said, his tone dispassionate and matter-of-fact, pulling her up from her doubts more effectively than any amount of reassurance would have done. "He'll be at the dinner tonight. I'll tell him we need to talk to him. I'm sure he can make a few phone calls and get some information for you.

Do you have your mother's social security number? Her driver's license?''

''Yes, I do, but I haven't been able to find out anything using them. Everyplace I call, they won't tell me anything.''

''You'd be surprised what doors a license to practice law can open.''

For just a moment a feeling of resentment washed over her, resentment that *other* people had more advantages than she did. *Other* people had access to things she'd never have access to.

But that was her mother's programming. Intellectually, she knew such an attitude wasn't right, that each person had individual skills. She should be grateful that someone could obtain information she couldn't. She had her own set of skills.

And if knowledge of the Dewey decimal system could ever save a life, she'd be able to utilize those skills. She had a brief, ridiculous flash of an emergency scene, red lights flashing, ambulance attendants kneeling beside a prone body, a house on fire in the background...and her standing to one side explaining where books could be found on fire fighting and CPR.

Okay, so maybe her skills weren't exactly on a par with those of a lawyer or a doctor...like Lucas.

At best, she might be able to thwack a victim on the chest with that book on CPR.

''Are you going to let me in on the joke? Anything that can produce such a gorgeous smile must be pretty funny.''

Sara felt the hot blood rise to her face again. Damn...darn, she immediately corrected, gulping, automatically expecting a reprimand from June Martin who'd frequently seemed able to read her rebellious thoughts.

But June wasn't here.

After a brief moment of sadness at the loss of the only family she'd ever known, Sara permitted herself to boldly think the swearword again, this time without censorship.

Damn!

"Damn!" She said it aloud.

Lucas blinked twice, and Sara's smile died as the familiar cold dread spread over her.

Lucas's eyes clouded. He rose from his chair and covered the short space between them in one stride then sat beside her and took her hands in his. "What did that woman do to you? Was she abusive?"

"No, of course not. She was strict, that's all."

"Strict how? Beatings?"

Sara tried to look away, to pull her hands away, but he held both her gaze and her hands firmly. "Spankings, switchings, but mostly she was just stern."

"Well, she's not here anymore, and it's okay if you want to swear a blue streak. I've already done it a couple of times today. It's your turn. *Damn's* a good place to start. Kind of an all-purpose curse. It rolled off your tongue very nicely a minute ago, except it sounded entirely too happy, and you smiled too big. Let's try it again with a little more anger. Damn!"

Sara laughed, then made an effort to turn her facial features into a more severe expression. "Damn!" she repeated.

"Damn!" Lucas said again, the corners of his mouth turning up.

"Damn! Damn, damn, damn!"

Both of them burst into laughter.

Lucas still held her hands with one of his while he lifted the other to push her newly acquired curls back from her face. "I don't think I've ever heard anyone swear with so much enjoyment."

She started to laugh again, but something in Lucas's dark gaze stopped the sound before it could rise more than halfway up her throat.

His fingers lingered along her cheek and down her chin, his touch whisper-soft yet leaving a trail of sparks in its wake. His scents of expensive cologne and masculinity swirled around her, blending with the eucalyptus and leather and producing a heady sensation. Or maybe it was only Lucas's touch that produced that heady sensation, that set her mind whirling and her body tingling.

He lifted his other hand to her face, pushing back the hair on that side, too, then cupping her chin in his palm.

Her hair! Sara's heart knotted painfully. Her hair and makeup made her look exactly like Analise. Lucas was seeing his fiancée. It wasn't Sara Martin he was touching and gazing at in that hungry way. It was Analise's look-alike.

"Sara," he whispered, and she felt a thrill pulse through her at his use of her name, not Analise's. "You are so..."

She waited, not daring to breathe, for what he would say next. So like Analise? So much more attractive with her hair like Analise's?

"So tempting," he murmured. "And you aren't even aware of it."

Sara lost every last vestige of her contact with reality when he said that, when she knew that he was really seeing her and not Analise.

Lucas's lips descended to hers, and she responded to

him ravenously, leaning into him, losing herself in his kiss, as though she'd reached an oasis after long years of drought. His arms wrapped around her, pulling her close against the solidity of his body as his lips moved on hers, soft and firm, demanding and giving, and this strange world she'd stumbled into seemed suddenly a warm, familiar place.

Her heart raced wildly in rhythm with his while her entire body pulsed to that new yet ancient and elemental rhythm. Her own arms slid around him, her fingers on his back moving over the soft fabric of his shirt, testing the ridges of muscle beneath, each one a new discovery yet familiar on a deeper level.

His tongue teased her lips, and she parted them, the wave of desire that overwhelmed her giving her an instinctive perception of this ritual. Her breasts against his chest seemed to swell as if reaching for him, yearning to be even closer, and the knowledge that she was alone in a house with this man only heightened her sensitivity.

Her entire body vibrated against him with pulsing desire.

No, actually, his body was vibrating against hers, especially in a small area at her waist where he held her tightly to him, where she could feel a hard bulge.

Her heart raced faster at the implication. But…were arousals off to the side like that? Did they have sharp corners? Did they vibrate?

He groaned and slowly withdrew from her, his lips leaving hers with a series of small, regretful kisses.

"My pager," he said. "I'm sorry." He reached between them and extracted the small, vibrating object. "I have to call the hospital."

His pager.

She wanted to laugh at her own ignorance, but somehow she no longer felt like laughing.

He left her sitting on the leather sofa whose surface now seemed cold instead of pleasantly cool. She shivered and wrapped her arms around herself as she watched Lucas cross the elegant room with an easy stride and pick up the telephone.

She felt abandoned and guilty. The guilt was easy to understand. She'd just kissed the fiancé of a woman who might be her sister. The feeling of abandonment, however, was irrational.

She couldn't be abandoned by someone she'd never possessed. Lucas had kissed her, not made a commitment to her.

She studied him as he spoke authoritatively into the phone.

He was a doctor, a respected member of the community. He had position and—she looked around her at the leather furniture, the paintings, the hardwood floors accented with expensive rugs—money.

Perhaps her mother hadn't been wrong about everything.

Lucas was engaged to a woman from his socioeconomic strata. He might kiss another woman who had no such standing, who didn't have money or family or heritage or even a real birth certificate, but he'd walk away from that woman, from that kiss, completely untainted.

Walk away and call the hospital, rejoin his world.

He hung up the phone, turned back to her and smiled. "Sorry about that interruption," he said. "I just had to approve some medication for a patient."

Sara tensed, wondering if she'd have the strength to reject him if he attempted to resume the kiss. She knew she should, but her body was screaming with a different knowledge.

To her relief and regret, he stopped with the coffee table still between them, his hands in the pockets of his stylish slacks.

"I'm going to change clothes and then we'll go on to the restaurant. It's getting close to time to go."

She nodded her agreement and he left the room.

Yes, he could kiss her passionately then walk away...to marry Analise.

Chapter Six

The first time Lucas had dined at the Lakeside Country Club as a guest of Ralph Brewster's, he'd been awed by the elegant decor and the hushed atmosphere that spoke of old money and decades of tradition. Over the years, as a member and regular visitor, he'd become accustomed to all of it and had forgotten that initial reaction of wonder.

Tonight he found it again through Sara's eyes.

As they followed the hostess across the main dining room to the private room where the rehearsal dinner was to be held, Sara exuded an almost palpable sense of wonder. Lucas looked around him, noticing anew all the dark, polished wood, the leaded glass in the windows, the sparkle from the crystal chandeliers, the smell of freshly baked bread that almost overpowered the faint scents of lemon oil and tradition.

He knew from his own experience that she'd also be nervous. His first time here he'd been certain he'd make such a huge faux pas that not only would Ralph demand he return all the scholarship money, but the country-club officials would clutch him by the nondesigner label in his sport coat and drag him off the premises.

Because he knew Sara felt that way too—knew it and sensed it as much as he sensed the wonder, as if he was somehow attuned to her—he took her hand and gave it a reassuring squeeze.

She smiled up at him, and he realized reassurance hadn't been the only reason he'd taken her hand. He'd wanted to touch her again.

What the hell was happening to him? He was engaged to Analise, a woman he cared about and didn't want to hurt, a woman whose family he cared about. He wanted to marry Analise. Okay, so she was a little unpredictable, but the way he felt about her was very predictable—safe and undemanding.

He didn't want this seductive feeling of needing to touch another person so badly that nothing else mattered, of being so attuned to that person, he could almost read her mind. Even beyond the blatant question of loyalty to his fiancée, he didn't want to experience that overpowering passion that robbed a person of his common sense.

He didn't want it, and yet at the same time yearned for it, couldn't get enough of it. Even while one side of him stood looking on in horror and dismay, the other side beamed down at Sara and gloried in the way she beamed back at him.

Whistles and catcalls greeted them as they entered the private dining room. "All right, you two," someone called, "enough of that goo-goo-eyes nonsense! It's time to eat!"

Lucas looked up to see the wedding party seated at

a long table, watching Sara and him. Great. Caught in
the act of being an idiot.

The pianist in the corner broke into a jazzed-up ver-
sion of the wedding march and everybody clapped.

With a final squeeze, Lucas turned loose of Sara's
hand and pulled out a chair for her then took a seat
beside her, next to Ralph who sat at the head of the
table.

The waiter appeared, and filled their wineglasses.

As the meal progressed, Lucas noticed that Sara
watched him the way he'd watched Ralph on his first
visit, taking up the appropriate fork or spoon only after
he did, mimicking his actions carefully. Her first sip of
the dry wine brought a startled grimace to her un-
guarded face. Her adoptive mother's strict discipline
had doubtless included a prohibition on alcoholic bev-
erages. Nevertheless, she gamely continued, matching
him bite for bite and drink for drink.

Now he knew how Henry Higgins must have felt. Not
that Sara was, by any stretch, as uneducated as Eliza
Doolittle. But her unworldly naiveté, the way she
looked to him for guidance, added another element to
her inexplicable attraction.

Gradually, he noticed, she seemed to relax, making
small talk and laughing with her attendant, Linda, who
sat next to her. However, most of her comments were
quiet observations to him concerning the incredible
meal that the rest of the party consumed, he suspected,
without really tasting. They were all accustomed to
what, for Sara, was a new experience.

And just as he'd seen the main room through Sara's
eyes, so Lucas tasted the food with a renewed palate.
The stuffed mushrooms, the salmon with dill sauce, the

fresh asparagus, a different wine with every course—in all of it he tasted subtle flavors he hadn't noticed before.

Even the soft strains of elevator-type music that came from the pianist seemed melodious and full, like a Beethoven concerto.

All his senses were heightened, receptive to the smallest stimulus, as if Sara's presence, her touch, somehow broke down walls.

She was like a drug.

For a moment his medical training led him on a mental search of drugs that could cause such an effect, but he came up with nothing that could create such a euphoric, alert sensation with no side effects.

Well, actually Sara's presence in his life could have all sorts of potentially dangerous side effects. If he let it. But he wasn't going to let it.

The waiter set two plates of dessert in front of Sara.

"Your favorite," Lucas exclaimed, cueing her. "A double portion of chocolate soufflé with chocolate rum sauce."

"It looks delicious," Sara said, and Lucas could only hope she didn't hate chocolate or wasn't allergic to it. "Thank you, D-dad and…Mom," she stuttered, and though she had trouble addressing Ralph and Clare as *Mom* and *Dad,* nevertheless her voice was warm when she spoke.

"You're welcome, sweetheart."

The waiter served single portions to everyone else.

Only after Lucas took a bite did Sara begin to eat her dessert.

As he watched nervously from the corner of his eye, uncertain if she'd like the deeply chocolate flavor, Sara closed her eyes as if in ecstasy. "Oh, my! This is the most wonderful thing I've ever tasted!"

One more thing she and Analise had in common.

How could any two people be so much alike and so different?

And how could those same two women affect him in such totally different ways?

He couldn't keep his eyes off Sara as she ate both desserts with every bit as much gusto as Analise displayed when she was on a chocolate binge. But, like everything else about them, Sara's actions were different. Her lips, jaw and throat moved in a sensual way, transforming the act of eating into an erotic performance, making him ache to kiss her again, to taste the chocolate on her lips and tongue and to feel those lips moving against his.

She finished the second soufflé and sat back, turning to him with a satisfied smile and sparkling eyes. "That was incredible. Sure beats bologna sandwiches and chocolate cupcakes."

Her voice was just a shade loud, and though he couldn't help smiling at her, he lifted a cautionary finger to his lips. Analise had probably eaten her share of prepackaged cupcakes, but he doubted she'd ever had a bologna sandwich. /

A waiter removed his own dessert practically untasted. But that was okay. He'd tasted every bite of Sara's right along with her.

Sara looked across the room, then back to him, her pretty features marred by a frown. "Is he going to eat?"

He looked around the table at the obviously satiated people. "Who?"

"The piano player."

"I guess so, after he leaves here."

Her frown deepened. "Will he have the same thing we did?"

"I don't know. Probably not."

"But that's horrible! He has to sit there and watch all of us eat and smell this wonderful food, then go home to a bologna sandwich and chocolate cupcake?"

Lucas had never thought of that before, but she was right. They were treating the man as if he weren't there, as if he didn't matter. It had taken someone unaccustomed to the traditions of the country-club set to point it out, someone with a kind, caring heart.

"Analise—" Ralph began, and Lucas realized Sara had spoken loudly enough for him to hear.

"It's okay," Lucas assured Ralph, then lifted a hand to summon a waiter. "Would you please see that the pianist has the same meal we had and put it on my account?"

"Certainly, sir."

Lucas watched the waiter leave. No questions were asked concerning the unusual request. Courtesy and respect. It sure beat the heck out of taunts and insults. He'd come a long way in Briar Creek, most of that way uphill, though sometimes he felt as though he still perched precariously atop that hill, poised to topple over at the slightest infraction.

No matter what, he wasn't going to let that happen. He couldn't let that happen.

Sara laid a soft hand on his. "Thank you," she said, and his world shifted. Suddenly nothing else mattered except the happiness in her green eyes.

He must be on drugs after all.

They'd had an awful lot of wine during the meal. Maybe he was intoxicated.

Sara's fingers were warm on his. Her scent of magnolia blossoms caressed him.

He was definitely intoxicated, though he wasn't sure it had anything to do with the wine.

The final course was champagne.

Ralph stood and lifted his glass. "Never has that old cliché been more true, that Clare and I aren't losing a daughter, we're gaining a son. I'd like to propose a toast. To our daughter, Analise, the light of our lives, the one who's made us crazy and kept us sane, aged us twenty years and kept us young, who's made our lives worth living, and to Lucas, my future son-in-law, my partner and best golfing buddy because he's so bad I can always beat him." He lifted his glass. "May you both always be as happy as you've made Clare and me. And, Lucas, may your golf game continue to be lousy and may you always live in a ranch-style home so Analise can't slide down the banister."

Everyone at the table laughed, then drank the toast.

Lucas held his glass to his lips, but he couldn't swallow. Even one sip under such deceitful circumstances would probably strangle him.

He set his glass down and turned to Sara to see how she was handling the situation.

Much better than he was, apparently. She was smiling, her eyes dancing…and her glass half-empty. Maybe he should caution her about the champagne on top of all those dinner wines.

He leaned close to her, but Tom Jenkins, his best man, stood and proposed another toast.

After that, the waiter refilled everyone's glass, and Linda, Analise's maid of honor, rose. Her toast ended with a request that Analise sing something.

"Oh, no, I can't!" Sara protested as a clamor rose around the table applauding the request.

Lucas laid a protective arm around her shoulders.

"She's had a long day. We all have. Let's call it a night."

"'Summertime,'" Clare said, her quiet but decisive voice cutting through the noise. "Do 'Summertime,' sweetheart. The song you learned because I sang it to you so much. Sing it for me tonight."

Sara turned to him, her face a study in quiet panic.

Lucas started to protest, to insist that Analise needed to leave, not sing, but Ralph's voice stopped him.

"Please, baby? You won't be our little girl for much longer."

Sara looked from him back to Clare, then to Lucas's amazement, she nodded.

The pianist ran through a few bars of the song and Sara slid her chair back.

Lucas grabbed her hand as she stood. "Analise, you've been under a lot of stress today. You don't need to sing. You might forget the words or something."

She looked down at him with that same glazed expression he'd seen on her face when Clare had insisted she go home from the church with Ralph and her.

He released her hand. The good thing was, if she made a total mess of the song, everyone would just attribute it to one of Analise's capers.

Sara spoke softly to the pianist, then stood primly beside him, her hands at her sides. Yes, she could easily be Analise preparing to be wild and outrageous, except when Analise pretended to be serious, she always had a spark of laughter in her eyes, not a spark of terror.

Right on cue, she began to sing in a subdued but melodious voice. He certainly had to give her credit. It took a lot of guts to do something like that when she was terrified.

He supposed that, having had no loving parents of

her own, she was extremely susceptible to the adoration Analise's parents offered and would, consequently, do anything they asked. Agreeing to sing in front of everybody when she was almost painfully shy was a testament to how desperately she wanted to please Ralph and Clare. The champagne might have given her a little false courage. Nevertheless, he had to get her out of this mess he'd gotten her into before she became so accustomed to that adoration that leaving would hurt her.

This masquerade was having unexpected, adverse effects. He was afraid Sara was getting confused, becoming entangled in the parental love Ralph and Clare had for Analise. Thank goodness he had no insane passion for Analise that Sara could get confused about. He and Analise were friends. He and Sara were friends. That was safe. Nobody was going to get hurt on that one.

He watched as she gradually relaxed and began to sing with more feeling, more animation. She sounded incredibly like Analise. She tilted her head back and closed her eyes on the high notes the way Analise did. Yet he knew he'd be able to tell the difference even if both women stood side by side.

No, his quiet, sane feelings for Analise weren't going to confuse Sara and cause her problems.

But his feelings for Sara were a different story. He had to get away from her before he did more damage to her than Ralph and Clare possibly could. She was so fragile, so vulnerable, that she could easily be hurt.

He stole a quick glance at Ralph to see how he was reacting since he was the one Sara thought was suspicious of her. Ralph looked completely enraptured. And no wonder. Sara was really getting into that song, almost as if Analise's spirit possessed her.

She had obviously had too much champagne. He should have paid more attention, warned her.

As she belted out the final chorus, she kicked off her shoes, angled a hip onto the piano, drew one bare foot up to the other knee and, as she sang the last note, spread her arms wide.

Just like Analise would have done.

Completely unlike Sara.

He had to get her out of there.

Everyone burst into applause as she finished the song. She smiled, took a bow, blew kisses.

Lucas charged up to her, took her arm and turned to face the others.

"It's been great fun! Thank you all for coming. And now I have to get my beautiful princess home before she turns into a pumpkin," he announced, urging her toward the door.

"We'll be home in a little while," Ralph called.

"It was the coach that turned into a pumpkin," Sara corrected quietly as Lucas hustled her out the door. "Cinderella turned back to—" she looked up at him, her eyes wide "—a poor girl. A chambermaid."

A poor girl. A chambermaid. Her own words echoed in Sara's mind as she waited with Lucas for the valet to bring the shabby car that her pumpkin had always been.

Lucas was ashamed of her. She'd embarrassed him in front of his friends.

"I'm sorry," she said as soon as he went around and climbed into the seat beside her.

He turned toward her, his expression unreadable in the darkness. "Sorry? For what?"

She dropped her gaze to her hands as they clutched

each other in a death grip in her lap. "For...you know...making a fool of myself in front of everybody."

Lucas cupped her chin and forced her to look at him. Even in the dim light, she could see his teeth flashing white in a wide smile. "Sara, you were wonderful. I'm *proud* of you. I know you were scared, and that makes it even more incredible that you did it and did it so well."

Her heart swelled with happiness at his words and she wanted desperately to believe him.

He put the car into gear and started down the long driveway.

"Then why were you so anxious to get me out of there?" she asked quietly, not wanting to hear the answer but needing to anyway.

"Well..." He hesitated and cleared his throat.

She braced herself for whatever he might say.

"I was afraid you'd had, uh, a little too much to drink."

That certainly wasn't what she'd expected. "Too much to drink? You thought I needed to go to the ladies' room?"

He guided the car onto the street and gave her a quick glance. "The ladies' room?" Then, as if comprehension had finally reached him, he laughed, a deep, rich sound like the chocolate syrup on that soufflé.

"No," he said, "not the ladies' room. Not that kind of drink. Too much wine and champagne."

"You thought I was *inebriated?*"

"It crossed my mind."

She leaned back, taking her gaze from him, looking instead into the wide, dark world passing outside the car, a world she knew so little of. She rolled down her window to let the air come in and clear her head, but instead it brought the scents of honeysuckle and jasmine, scents that tantalized her with promises of the sweetness of that world…the world where Lucas lived.

"Maybe I am," she said. "I've never had champagne or wine or anything else alcoholic before. What's it like to be drunk?"

"Oh, light-headed, euphoric, you lose your inhibitions."

"Then I must be because I feel all those things." Though she had been feeling them ever since she'd met him, not just tonight. Certainly his kisses had made her feel all those things, especially the part about losing her inhibitions and kissing him back.

"I was a little surprised when you got up and sang."

"Me, too," she admitted. "Before tonight, I'd have sworn I could never have found the courage to get up in front of a roomful of people and sing. I've never sung anywhere alone except in the shower. My music teacher in high school asked me to do a solo in the class talent show, but I couldn't. Yet when I was up there tonight, I wondered why I hadn't done it years ago."

"Why didn't you? You must have practiced that song a lot or you wouldn't have had it down so perfectly. In fact, you must have a fairly big repertoire. I can't believe Clare just happened to pick the one song you know."

"It's one of my favorites. I used to fantasize that my mother was singing it to me, that I had the rich father and beautiful mother in the song instead of no father and a mother who…well, I'm sure she loved me, but I don't think she liked me very much." She pulled her gaze back to the interior of her car, away from that dark, mysterious world outside that drew her with an allure she'd never noticed before, that promised all sorts of secrets waiting for her to explore, all sorts of new experiences that would yield more of the intoxicating sensations she'd had today. Not that there was anything wrong with wanting to learn more about the world outside her tiny sphere. The problem was that most of those intoxicating sensations involved Lucas, a man to whom she had no rights both by dint of his being engaged and because he was miles away from her. He belonged to a country club, knew which forks to use and when to use them, could take care of her request for dinner for the piano player with a wave of his hand.

She shoved that part of the excitement of the day aside and focused on the parts she could deal with.

"The reason I could never sing in public was because my mother always made me feel self-conscious when anyone paid attention to me. Yet tonight I had the attention of everybody in that room, and I loved it. I felt light-headed and euphoric and exhilarated. If that's how it feels to be inebriated, I can see why so many people do it."

Lucas's low chuckle filled the car and surrounded her, like a caress. "You sound pretty sober and lucid to me. I'm actually not sure how much the alcohol had to do with your performance."

She thought about that. She hadn't had anything to drink before Lucas kissed her except iced tea, so there must have been something else going on besides alcohol consumption.

"Then how do you explain it?"

"I don't know. Maybe you felt freer because you were pretending to be Analise. Maybe you got into the role so completely, you did what she'd do. A lot of professional actresses are actually quite shy until they assume a role."

"Did I sing like Analise?" *Did I kiss like Analise?* She hadn't been pretending to be Analise when she'd kissed him, though she hadn't felt like Sara, either.

"If I hadn't known better, I'd have sworn it was Analise up there. You looked like her, you sang like her, your gestures were like hers. Even that last bit where you kind of sat on the piano and threw up your arms…that was exactly like Analise. This theory of yours that you two might be twins, as improbable as it sounds, I'm beginning to think it's possible. There doesn't seem to be any other explanation."

Sara turned away from Lucas and looked out the window again. Surely she must be affected by the champagne. Otherwise how was it possible for her to feel intense happiness and devastating sadness at the same time?

That she might be Analise's twin, that she might have a sister, a real family was more than she'd ever dared to wish for.

Yet at the same time, she realized that Lucas was proud of her not because she had done something commendable but only because she was so like his fiancée. When he'd kissed her, he'd really been kissing Analise.

Not that she had any reason or right to be upset about that.

But she was.

Sara suddenly realized that they weren't anywhere in the vicinity of the Sleep Well Motel. "Where are we going?" she asked as Lucas drove through the open security gate that led to the Brewsters' house. That was a little odd, she thought, that they left the gate open when they were gone. Maybe it was more for show than actual safety. If June Martin had had a security gate, she'd have kept it locked all the time.

Nevertheless, they weren't supposed to be there. She couldn't possibly go back into that place that both beguiled and taunted her with its sense of home and family.

"I'm taking you—oh! I wasn't thinking." Lucas stopped in front of the garage and dropped his forehead into his hand. "Damn! We didn't make any excuses for your—I mean, for Analise's leaving town. What a tangled web we weave!" He leaned back and shook his head then looked at Sara, a rueful smile stretching his lips. "I'm sorry. I had no idea things were going to get so complicated. I think some of Analise's impulsiveness must have rubbed off on me that I ever came up with such a crazy scheme. You probably want to get back to your motel room, don't you?"

She nodded. "Yes, I need to." *Back to that impersonal room that belonged to nobody, back to her real life where she belonged to nobody and could get all these foolish yearnings stuffed back into their proper compartments.*

"I'll think of something to tell Ralph and Clare. Maybe have Linda call and say Analise is spending the night with her and then tomorrow that she's going out of town. Linda'll think Analise and I are—you know."

Even in the dim glow from the yard lights, Sara could discern the dark blush that spread over Lucas's tanned face. She ducked her head to hide what she knew would be a much brighter crimson on her pale features at the thought of the *you know* that Linda would expect Analise and Lucas to be doing.

"I really appreciate all you've done for me," Lucas said. "I promise to reciprocate. I'll call Tom tomorrow and arrange for you to meet with him on Monday."

"Thank you." He was saying goodbye. She was never going to see him again.

Unless Analise did prove to be her sister.

Maybe they'd invite her to the wedding.

Lucas would be her brother-in-law.

She'd be *Aunt Sara* to their kids.

"Sara?"

She looked up at him. "What?"

"Are you all right?"

"Of course. Why wouldn't I be?"

"I don't know. You seemed kind of sad."

She shook her head and forced herself to smile. "I'm just tired. It's been a long day."

"Yeah, it has." He fiddled with the key but didn't turn it. "I really appreciate...I said that already, didn't I?"

"Yes."

"Well, I'd better get you to your motel room." He continued to stare at her but made no move to leave. The fragrance of roses drifted through her open window, their scent much more intoxicating than the champagne they'd had earlier. Or maybe it was only Lucas's nearness that was so intoxicating. "Actually, since we're in your car, I guess you'd better take *me* home and then go on to your motel."

The end was approaching. She'd leave Lucas at his home, then drive herself to that impersonal motel room.

Bright light flooded the car.

Sara spun around to see headlights pulling up behind them.

"It's Ralph and Clare," Lucas said. "We're trapped. You're trapped. I'm sorry."

Sara spared a fleeting thought for Lucas, that he didn't sound sorry. They could have escaped, but he'd lingered. Was he as reluctant to part from her as she from him? She knew that couldn't be right, but she had no time to think about it now.

The rest of her thoughts whirled around dizzily, so fast she couldn't quite focus on any one. Was she distressed Ralph and Clare had come back, upsetting her plans to return to the motel? Was she terrified that she'd have to spend the night here and risk getting caught? Did she feel guilty about lying again to Ralph and Clare, taking their affection and parenting under false pretenses?

All those things, certainly, but a tiny, shameful part of her was thrilled at the thought of going into that big, intimidating house, into that warm, caring family.

"They think I borrowed this car," Lucas reminded her, "and that yours—I mean, Analise's—is at my house. We could tell them I'm taking you to get your car, and then you could disappear."

Of course. The answer was simple. She could get away easily. She wasn't trapped after all. This whole ordeal was over.

Thank goodness.

So what was wrong with her that she didn't feel relieved?

In the bright glare, Lucas's tanned skin seemed washed out and pale, his eyes a stark contrast, dark, fathomless wells of midnight.

"Or," he said, his casual tone belying the intensity in those eyes, "it would be a lot easier, if you could stand to carry on this masquerade just a little longer, for you to go upstairs and spend the night in Analise's room, then I could come and get you for church in the morning."

"Easier," she repeated, trying to discern his thoughts

from the expression in his eyes, but it was too dark. Was he saying that because he wanted her to stay, because he wanted to see her again in the morning? "Yes, that would be a lot easier."

She must still be drunk to agree to that plan...to *want* to agree to that plan, to want to stay another night with Ralph and Clare, to want to see Lucas again.

Well, she couldn't. No matter how much she wanted to, it wasn't right. Ralph, Clare and Lucas all belonged to Analise. They weren't even hers to borrow.

She opened her mouth to protest her own capitulation, to declare that she couldn't possibly do any such thing, that she wanted to take Lucas to his home and go back to her motel room.

"Are you coming in, sweetheart?" Clare's voice came through the open window behind her.

"Ah, young love," Ralph added, leaning down beside his wife to peer in at them. "You're going to see her again in just a few hours, my boy. Let her get a little sleep tonight."

Lucas's lips formed the word *please,* and Sara was helpless against the three of them, against her own foolish, self-destructive need for the three of them.

She got out of the car. Clare looped an arm around her waist and Ralph laid his across her shoulder.

"I'll see you tomorrow," Lucas called.

Such an exquisite, bittersweet feeling of belonging, of having a family...and a lover.

All a sham.

And she'd better keep that in mind.

She was flirting with danger, coming precipitously close to the temptation of letting herself believe in the charade for one exquisite, shining moment. But if she ever did, that fleeting moment of ecstasy would make the rest of her real life unbearable.

Already she ached to feel Lucas's arms around her again, to see him smiling at her proudly, to know he cared enough to want to fulfill her wishes by arranging dinner for the piano player.

All of which belonged to Analise, the woman she looked enough like that even Analise's fiancé became confused.

Sara couldn't afford to let herself become confused, couldn't afford to believe she really was Analise, not even for that one tempting moment.

She steeled herself to get through the night and the next day without feeling.

Chapter Seven

A ray of sunlight coming between the motel-room curtains that didn't quite meet in the middle woke Sara early Monday morning. She sat up and looked around the dingy room. It wasn't that much worse than the places she'd lived all her life with June Martin, yet today it had a forlorn appearance.

Yesterday morning she'd awakened in Analise's cheerful bedroom with Clare stroking her hair back from her face and urging her to hurry so she'd have time for breakfast before church.

They'd gone back to the big, overpowering church where she'd been to the rehearsal on Saturday...where she'd walked down the aisle to meet Lucas. On Sunday she'd sat between Clare and Lucas with Ralph on the end. She'd stood to sing and knelt to pray and been thoroughly enchanted by the entire event, so unlike the infrequent disorderly prayer meetings she'd attended with her mother. The preacher at Analise's church didn't even shout.

He did talk about deceit, however, and she'd wanted to slide under the pew and shrink to a speck of dust then disappear into the thick carpet. Lucas had laid his arm around her shoulder, a reassuring gesture, and she'd survived by reminding herself that her deceit was in a good cause, to avoid worrying Analise's family.

After the service, lots of people had come up to the Brewsters, to Lucas and to her in the mistaken assumption she was Analise. Once more, Sara had had to fight to prevent herself from absorbing all this goodwill and friendship like a dry sponge, from believing it belonged to her.

As they stood on the sidewalk outside, Lucas had told Clare and Ralph that she was coming home with him to get her car and was then going to Dallas to attend a conference on butterflies.

"Entomology," Sara had supplied.

"A conference on Sunday evening?" Ralph had questioned.

"Early Monday morning," Lucas had improvised.

"Very early," Sara had verified.

It had taken all her fortitude to resist Ralph and Clare's efforts to get her to come home long enough to eat lunch and pack a bag and to resist Lucas's invitation as they drove away to take her out to lunch.

"Someone might see us and tell Ralph and Clare that Analise didn't really leave town," she'd explained. It was the truth. She didn't want to hurt them, to have them think their daughter had lied to them. But the biggest reason she couldn't go with him was the same reason she couldn't spend any more time with Ralph and Clare—because she wanted to much too badly. She wasn't Analise, and this pretending was getting a little too real, a little scary.

As she climbed out of bed and headed for the shower, Sara resolved to get back on track, to make a concerted effort to discover her own identity and let go of Analise's. She'd go to the bank this morning then spend the rest of the day in the library looking for any mention of June Martin.

Perhaps by then Analise would have returned and she could meet this woman who looked so much like her and had everything she'd ever wanted. If they were twins, they could work together to find their real parents, though Analise might be less anxious than she. Analise had parents whether or not they'd actually given their DNA to her.

Sara paused in front of the splotchy bathroom mirror.

How was she going to do any searching in this town without being mistaken for Analise?

The minister at church had been right. Deceit was a bad deal all around.

She could braid her hair again instead of wearing it the way Analise wore hers.

But that hadn't stopped Lucas from thinking she was Analise.

She needed a disguise.

She giggled at that thought, but then recalled Lucas's words from Saturday night.

Maybe you felt freer because you were pretending to be Analise. Maybe you got into the role so completely, you did what she'd do. A lot of professional actresses are actually quite shy until they assume a role.

If she got a brown wig, a pair of glasses and a severe suit, she could pretend to be someone else when she went to the bank, someone who had the right to ask for information about June Martin.

In fact, she didn't even have to use her real name or

reason for looking for June. She'd seen television shows where clever private detectives had a variety of business cards printed up so they were prepared for whatever occasion arose. All she needed was access to a computer.

The town of Tyler was only about an hour away. She could drive over there and buy what she needed, then come back and get busy.

Sara slid into the shower with a renewed sense of purpose and a dash of excitement over the idea of being someone else, someone who wore glasses and a severe suit and brooked no nonsense from recalcitrant bank officers.

It was early afternoon before Sara walked through the door of the First National Bank of Briar Creek. No one looked up. No one seemed to notice her, and for a moment timidity overpowered her, urging her back out the door.

No, Sara Martin was timid. Mary Miller, investigator for Preferential Life, was bold, even a little arrogant.

She smoothed the slim black skirt of her suit, pushed her glasses up on her nose and touched her short, straight brown wig to be sure it was still in place. The glasses, low-powered reading lenses, as close to nothing as she could find, gave the room a fuzzy, unreal quality. That should make this even easier.

In her Mary Miller walk, she strode up to the information desk and flipped out one of the cards she'd printed that morning.

"I'm looking for a former employee," she said briskly—just the way Mary Miller, insurance investigator, would. "A June Martin. She worked here around 1970 or 1971." Sara Martin had called from Deauxville,

Missouri, and said, *She might have worked here.* Mary Miller spoke with certainty.

And, whereas Sara Martin had been given the runaround and brushed off, Mary Miller was ushered to the office of George Fremont, the bank's president, a man who'd refused to take Sara Martin's phone calls.

As Sara shook his pulpy, damp hand, then sat in a chair in front of his desk, she marveled that she'd ever been intimidated by the idea of this short, pudgy, fuzzy, balding man. Of course, he wouldn't be so fuzzy without her glasses.

"Would you like a cup of coffee?" he asked.

"No, thank you. Just some information. June Martin is the beneficiary of a one-hundred-thousand life-insurance policy, and this is the only address we have for her."

"June Martin." He folded his hands over his rounded stomach. "Seems like we had someone else inquiring about her not long ago."

"Yes, we had a clerk in our company call here, but she wasn't given any information, so they sent me down."

"Yeah, that's all it was. A phone call." He picked up his phone and asked someone to bring him the personnel records for 1970 and 1971.

"Your job must be interesting," he said while they waited.

"It is," she agreed. She'd been three different people over the last three days! "But I'm sure being a bank president is quite fascinating, too."

He shrugged and spread one hand toward his paperstrewn desk. "It's a living. The company moved me here from Dallas when they took over. It was a good promotion, but this town sure doesn't compare with

Dallas. Where are you from?'' He consulted her card. ''Kansas City. I've been to conventions there. Nice place.''

She shrugged, too, using only one shoulder. It seemed more sophisticated that way. ''It's all right. Cold in the winter and hot in the summer.''

He nodded gravely as though she'd made a sage observation rather than a dumb statement that applied to ninety percent of the country.

After several interminable minutes of small talk, a woman brought a box of papers to Fremont's desk. ''This is 1971,'' she said. ''I'll be back in a minute with 1970.''

He lifted off the lid and scowled at what he saw. ''This was before we took over,'' he explained to Sara. ''They didn't have things computerized. Guess that's why, when your clerk called, nobody would tell her anything. This is going to be quite a job. Sorry.''

''No problem.''

''Why don't I put you in a private room down the hall and you can spend all the time you want going through these?''

Sara had to restrain herself from jumping up and down, from laughing out loud, from shouting. ''Thank you,'' she said primly.

Fremont stood and picked up the box, his face flushing with the effort.

Sara's heartbeat accelerated as she realized she was going to actually see the records of her mother's employment, find her mother's address in Briar Creek. She was on the verge of getting her first lead.

Soon she should have some concrete information to give Lucas's lawyer friend, Tom Jenkins.

Conceivably, by the end of the week, she might know

who her real mother was, why she'd given her up, if she wanted to have a relationship now…and whether Analise was her sister.

Having Sara come to his house Tuesday evening to meet with Tom Jenkins was the only logical way to do things, Lucas told himself as he tossed three steaks onto his patio grill. And fixing dinner for Tom and Sara was only hospitable. And logical. Sara couldn't risk being seen at a restaurant right now.

He went back inside to check on the baked potatoes and corn on the cob.

He hadn't seen Sara since she'd dropped him off after church on Sunday. He'd only talked to her once, to set up this meeting.

Okay, so he'd *thought* about her a couple of times. Several times, maybe. But only because the mystery of her resemblance to Analise was so intriguing.

Okay, so maybe part of it was hormones. Sara did have a way of sending his blood racing just by looking at him. But he wasn't some teenage kid, his whole life at the mercy of testosterone.

He wasn't his parents, so blinded by passion that he was ready to ruin his life.

Lucas added a few hearts of palm to the salad then tossed it with the dressing he'd finagled the chef at the country-club restaurant into selling him, the one Sara had raved about Saturday night. The guy had, however, adamantly refused to sell him chocolate soufflés, so he'd had to settle on getting a pan of brownies bursting with chocolate chips and pecans from the local bakery. Those, along with some rich vanilla ice cream and hot-fudge sauce should tickle Sara's chocolate fancy.

The doorbell rang, and he went to answer it.

Sara stood on his front porch wearing a white cotton blouse and calf-length denim skirt, her porcelain skin without makeup, looking gorgeous. The scent of roses seemed to surround her, calling up images from Saturday night when they'd sat in the dark in her car in front of the Brewsters' house...the way she'd looked, how desperately he'd wanted to hold her, to prevent her from leaving the Brewsters' house...from leaving his life.

Or maybe that memory was so strong it conjured up the scent of roses. Maybe the fragrance was only in his mind, an olfactory hallucination, something so inextricably linked to Sara that he was fated to smell roses every time she was near. She'd never be able to sneak up on him that way.

And he was forced to admit that of all the lies he'd told over the last few days, the biggest had been to himself...that he'd only invited Sara over because it was the logical thing to do, that he'd only thought about her because of her intriguing resemblance to Analise, that he wasn't going to let his hormones distract him or passion blind him.

Until he'd seen her standing there, he hadn't known how much he'd missed seeing her.

This was not a good sign.

This was a very, very bad sign.

He realized he'd been standing in his doorway, gaping at her for a long time. That wasn't a good sign, either.

"Come in," he said, stepping back.

She smiled and brushed past him. "Your neighbor has wonderful roses."

"He does?"

"Yes, can't you smell them?"

"Oh, yeah, those roses." Thank goodness the fragrance was real!

But why had he never noticed his neighbor's roses before?

Of course, he'd really never noticed the roses at the Brewsters' house before Saturday night.

He closed the door and turned around to face her, and suddenly he didn't know what to say. Or, to be more accurate, which of the thousand comments and questions darting through his mind he should say first.

"Would you like to go out on the patio? It's shady and cool. Well, not as cool as air-conditioning, of course. We could stay inside if you'd rather." Good grief! He hadn't stumbled all over himself like this since high school!

"I'd love to go outside," she said. "We never had air-conditioning at home, and I still find it a little chilly sometimes."

He touched her waist to guide her through the house. *Liar!* He could have directed her without touching her. He'd touched her because he wanted to.

Things were definitely on a downhill slide. Where had his loyalty to Analise gone? Apparently to the same place his common sense had disappeared to. He could only hope he'd stumble across them someday soon, hiding in a dark corner somewhere.

Thank goodness Tom was due to arrive any minute.

He showed Sara to the patio then came back inside to get glasses of iced tea for both of them.

After taking ice from the refrigerator, he stood with the door open, letting the frigid air roll over him. Not too many years ago when a patient had a complete mental breakdown, doctors would wrap him in icy sheets in an attempt to shock him back to reality. Maybe the refrigerator would work for him.

He reminded himself that he was engaged to Analise Brewster, he was happy to be engaged to Analise, he liked Analise, he liked Analise's parents, he didn't want to hurt Analise or Clare or Ralph. Analise had been hurt when that jerk she'd been involved with in college had let her down. He'd been there for her then, reassuring her and comforting her, and he wasn't about to be the one to cause her pain now.

Not to mention that he didn't want or need an all-consuming passion that could mess up his head and his life, the kind of passion that had sent his father to prison and wrecked his mother's life.

When he opened the patio door and stepped out, Sara smiled up at him from where she sat in a wrought-iron lawn chair. He tried to remember what it was he'd just reminded himself of, but the thoughts were pretty hazy. That cold certainly dissipated fast in the Texas heat.

"Thank you," she said, accepting the tea. "The steaks smell wonderful."

They did. The smell of steak and charcoal made his mouth water. Odd that he hadn't noticed it when he'd been out here before.

He turned the steaks, and they sizzled tantalizingly.

A breeze rustled through the trees and he looked up. Had the leaves on his cottonwood always made that melodic clicking sound when the wind blew?

Damn. This was that same kind of heightened-awareness thing he'd noticed on Saturday night, as though he was sensing everything in a brand-new way along with Sara.

Or because of Sara.

He plunked into a chair beside her. "How have you

been?'' he asked and wondered if it sounded as inane to her as it did to him.

"Fine," she said, sounding as though she really meant it. For the first time that evening Lucas looked closer, past his own desire or obsession or whatever it was Sara did to him. She was brimming with suppressed excitement. "I've been busy, doing some checking on my own."

"You mentioned on the phone that you'd been a couple of places. I thought you were concerned that people would see you and think Analise had returned."

"Oh, don't worry. I got up early Monday morning and drove over to Tyler to buy a short, brown wig, a pair of glasses and a power suit, then I came back here in disguise. Nobody could possibly have recognized me." Her eyes danced like the leaves overhead. She was obviously pleased with this latest masquerade. "It was kind of fun. Maybe I should be an actress. Like you said, when I'm pretending to be somebody else, I can do things I'd normally be terrified to do. And I'm certain I wasn't intoxicated yesterday or today. All I've had to drink is iced tea and sodas."

"I see." He was a little surprised that she'd been so daring, but she was pretty determined to discover her origins. That undoubtedly gave her an extra measure of courage. "So tell me all about it. Where did you go? What did you learn? Anything of interest? "

"Maybe. I was afraid I might be on the wrong track. Realistically, that pay stub in my mother's coat could have come from anywhere. She might have bought the coat at a used-clothing store. I talked to several people at the bank and nobody, not even a couple of people who worked there around the time I was born, remembered a June Martin. However, the president let me go through some very old records and even though I couldn't find her name anywhere, I did find—''

"The president? You got George Fremont to let you go through bank records?''

She sat erect, her expression shyly proud. "I couldn't get him to even speak to me on the phone when I called from Deauxville, so Monday I pretended to be an insurance investigator.''

"You what? And he took your word for it?'' Lucas couldn't decide if he was more astonished that Sara had done something so bold or that cynical, arrogant George Fremont had believed her.

"I was prepared. I stopped by a copy place while I was in Tyler and used a computer to print up a few business cards.'' She opened her purse, took out a half-dozen cards and handed them to Lucas.

"Mary Miller, Investigator, Preferential Life,'' he read. "Sandy Marshall, Agent, Federated Bureau of Investigations. Gayle Kasper, Private Investigator, Ace Detective Agency—Sara, you can't do this!''

"Why not?''

"Well, what if you get caught?''

"But those aren't real companies. I made them all up.''

"I know, but…'' He plowed shaky fingers through his hair.

"I wasn't assuming another identity with the intention of defrauding anyone. Besides, how could they catch me if those people and companies don't exist?''

She reached for her cards. He considered refusing to give them back, but she could always make more. He had to give her credit. She sure knew how to take an idea and run with it.

"Anyway, I went to the bank and told them I was

trying to find June Martin because she was the beneficiary of a hundred-thousand-dollar life-insurance policy, and this was the last address we had for her.'' She spoke primly and precisely, as though she'd done nothing out of the ordinary. That had probably made her all the more believable today.

Lucas rose and went to turn the steaks. This was all his fault. He'd taken a naive, unsophisticated girl—he looked over his shoulder at the swell of her breasts under that white cotton blouse, the trim ankle that peeked out from her skirt—and amended his thoughts. He'd taken a naive, unsophisticated *woman* and taught her to pretend to be somebody else. Taught her deceit. In spite of the admonitions of the minister on Sunday which had seemed to make her pretty uncomfortable at the time. She'd probably figured as long as she was doomed, she might as well go all the way.

He returned to his chair. ''Sara, we need to talk.''

Her eyes widened. She was obviously aware from his tone that something was wrong. Lucas swallowed the regret that rose in his throat, the desire to go to any lengths to avoid wounding someone so vulnerable.

What had happened to his sane, orderly life, his sane, orderly mind? He had to get a grip, stop this downward spiral into chaos, into Sara's green eyes…though the longer he looked, the harder it was to remember exactly why he had to stop.

The doorbell rang.

Tom.

Thank goodness.

Chapter Eight

Sara watched Lucas leave to answer the door. She'd been eager to share with him all she'd done—her innovative techniques as well as the possibility she'd uncovered her father's identity.

However, she could tell from the tone of his voice when he'd said they needed to talk that Lucas wasn't impressed, and he hadn't given her a chance to tell him about Albert Martin.

She sipped her tea, needing the cold liquid to moisten her mouth that had gone dry. But the ice had melted on top, diluting the drink to a weak, bitter flavor just as Lucas's attitude diluted her excitement.

What was the matter with her? Why had she thought, even for a fleeting moment, that her actions could be acceptable in Lucas's world? That he'd care about her tiny tidbit of information? And why did it matter anyway?

Lucas returned with a tall, blond man, and Sara stood.

''Sara Martin, Tom Jenkins,'' he said. ''Damn! The steaks are on fire!''

He dashed over to the grill, and Tom smiled at her, extending his hand. ''Pleased to meet you, Sara.''

She started to take his hand and realized hers was cold and wet from the condensation on her glass of tea. Now what? Did she wipe her hand on her skirt or give him a soggy handshake?

The lawyer with his immaculately cut and styled blond hair, his perfectly fitted trendy clothes and his air of confidence waited with outstretched hand. A few yards away the doctor with his immaculately cut and styled black hair, his perfectly fitted trendy clothes and his air of confidence tended steaks…any one of which probably cost more than most meals she and her mother had eaten.

Sara straightened her back and lifted her chin. Maybe she didn't know the appropriate etiquette, but she did have a little common sense. She swiped her hand down her denim skirt and offered it, dry, to Tom.

Tom clasped it with both of his, shook his head, laughed softly then shook his head again. ''This is unbelievable. Are you sure you're not Analise playing a joke on all of us? This is something she'd do, Lucas.''

Lucas came up behind him with a plate of charred steaks. ''She's not Analise,'' he said quietly. ''Trust me on this.''

His gaze met hers and she thought she saw a flash of regret before he turned away. Her heart twisted into a knot as cold as the glass she still held in her left hand, even though she told herself it was perfectly normal that he should regret she was there with him instead of his fiancée.

"I hope everybody likes their beef well done," he said, heading back inside with the steaks.

He passed the small kitchen table near a window and led them into the formal dining room where three places were set at the oval table of gleaming walnut. Sara sent up a short prayer of thanks that she recognized all the silverware tonight. Though she'd enjoyed the food at the country club, her pleasure had been tainted with the fear that she'd do something wrong. She hadn't known quite what to expect tonight and was relieved to see this meal was much more informal.

While they ate, Tom questioned her about her mother and assured her that they'd be able to find out all sorts of things from June Martin's social security number. If Sara's adoption hadn't been legal, that would present a few stumbling blocks, but if they could find where June Martin had lived when Sara was born, he could probably pull some strings and access local birth records for that time period.

When she told him about her ploy to obtain information from the bank, Tom laughed instead of getting upset the way Lucas had.

"Very clever," he said.

She blushed at the unaccustomed praise. "Nobody had ever heard of June Martin, but I did find a former employee named Albert Martin. That's the name listed as my father on my birth certificate." She tried to repress the excitement this discovery brought, trying not to get her hopes up then have them dashed to the ground again.

Lucas's wineglass thudded to the table as if he'd suddenly forgotten he held it, and allowed it to drop unnoticed. "Sara, that's wonderful! Why didn't you say something earlier?"

"You didn't give me a chance." She refrained from pointing out to him that he had been too busy being concerned with her methods, whether she'd been recognized, whether she'd done something illegal or embarrassing. After all, he had his standing in the community to think about while she had nothing. And that meant nothing to lose.

"Did you get an address for this Albert Martin?" Tom asked.

"I got the one the bank had, but he doesn't live there anymore. I went by the house today, and there's a young family there now." She wrapped both hands around her glass of tea, remembering the way she'd stood in front of the house, wondering if she'd been conceived there, if a man with red hair now gone white would open the door, recognize her when she pulled off her wig, exclaim how glad he was to find her after all these years and fold her into his embrace.

He hadn't, of course. She'd finally managed to work up enough courage to knock on the door, and a young woman with a baby in her arms and a toddler hanging on to her skirts had answered.

"They didn't buy the house from Albert Martin," she said, making herself continue to speak in an unemotional tone. "It's probably changed hands a couple of times. Albert Martin retired almost twenty years ago."

"Before the bank was sold and Fremont took over," Lucas said.

"Yes, so Mr. Fremont couldn't really tell me anything about him. Albert Martin's not in the Briar Creek phone book. I suppose he could be in Florida or Arizona or across the world by now." She unwound her fingers from her glass of iced tea, focusing her attention on that action. Nobody spoke the words she knew they must all be thinking. *Albert Martin could be dead by now.* "I got his social security number, so maybe Tom can find him with that."

Tom lifted an eyebrow and looked across the table to Lucas. "Smart girl."

Lucas leaned back in his chair, regarded her intently then smiled. "Yes," he agreed, "she is."

In spite of reliving the disappointment of her visit to Albert Martin's house, in spite of the fact that she didn't want her emotions to be so tied to Lucas's approval, Sara felt a warm glow. "After I left the bank," she continued, trying to ignore that misguided glow, "I went to the library to look at old newspaper stories, but I didn't find anything there. No June or Albert Martin. What I'm wondering now is whether Martin really was her last name. Maybe she took my real father's name, if his name is Albert Martin. To keep some of my identity."

"We'll find out," Tom reassured her. "With social security numbers, I can tell you what kind of formula they drank as babies."

She laughed, Tom's flippant remark easing some of the tension.

"What time period did you check in the newspapers?" Lucas asked.

"May, June and July, 1972. A month before and a month after my birthday."

Lucas leaned closer, his gaze intense, his half-eaten steak apparently forgotten. "When's your birthday?"

"June 25."

"Was the year 1972?"

"Yes. When's Analise's?" Her heart pounded loudly as she waited for him to say *June 25.*

"Not quite two months later. August 21, 1972."

Sara's hopes, already jerked up and down today, plummeted.

"Cancer the Crab and Leo the Lion," Tom said. "No wonder you can look so much like Analise but be more subdued. Cancer's a stable earth sign while Leo's an unpredictable fire sign."

Lucas's eyes never left hers. "Maybe. Or maybe June Martin lied about that, too. The year's the same, and the dates are awfully close, and it would seem this woman wasn't very well acquainted with the truth."

"Could be," Tom agreed. "If Sara's adoption wasn't legal, she might have worried constantly that the authorities would come and take her away so she changed everything. It's possible her birthday's the same as Analise's."

"It's possible Analise and I are twins," Sara said.

That Lucas and I are going to be brother- and sister-in-law.

She dropped her eyes, afraid he might see the dismay and guilt that idea brought. She busied herself with taking a final bite of baked potato. In spite of the sour cream and chives, it was dry and tasteless on her tongue.

Tom gave a low whistle. "Interesting theory. That would mean Analise is adopted, too."

"She doesn't look very much like either Ralph or Clare," Lucas commented.

"True."

"And while they're not as paranoid as Sara's mother was, they do worry a lot about Analise."

"They have a security gate," Sara said.

"Yes, they do," Lucas agreed. "A security gate they often leave open when they're gone and close when they're home, so it's not like they're worried about burglars."

Tom shook his head. "It just doesn't make sense. The Brewsters have money and position and power. They could legally adopt a child, any child."

"You tell me what *does* make sense. Sara comes to town looking so much like Analise, her own mother can't tell the difference, she's got an old pay stub from the local bank, Sara had a doll named Analise, Analise has a doll named Sara, they both studied bugs—"

"What?"

Sara laughed at Tom's confused expression. "He means entomology."

He grinned. "Oh, sure, the study of ents."

Sara laughed again. Tom was easy to talk to and seemed to accept her for who she was. Cancer the Crab, not Leo the Lion. Or maybe he saw the lion trapped inside her that seemed to be clawing its way to the surface lately.

"Sara and Analise even have the same heart-shaped birthmark on their left thigh," Lucas said, and Tom's eyes widened.

"He's kidding," Sara assured him, though she could feel the hot blood rising to her face at the suggestiveness of Lucas's remark.

"I am," Lucas admitted with a grin. "But they do wear the same size shoe, and they both love chocolate." He rose and slid back his chair. "Speaking of which, if I can trust you alone with the lovely Sara for a few minutes, I'll get our dessert."

Tom lifted his hands in a gesture of innocence. "I only turn into a wolf when there's a full moon."

Lucas gathered up their plates and left the room.

Tom turned to her with a wink. "That boy always did have trouble remembering what day it was. Obviously he doesn't know the full moon rises in another fifteen seconds. Keep an eye on the ears and let me know when hair starts to sprout. I try to get all my clothes off first so my pant legs won't drag on the ground and trip me.''

Sara laughed for a third time. "I'll never think of lawyer jokes the same way since I've met you," she said. "You probably wrote half of them."

"You should see my briefs." He winked, an impish grin stretching his lips. "The legal ones, I mean. The judge is always calling one of them a joke."

"You and Lucas are very different. He's so serious. How did you two meet?"

"At college in Austin. All the girls were following Lucas around, and I was following all the girls. I couldn't believe I'd found somebody who'd escaped from Briar Creek and wanted to go back."

"You wanted to leave? But you're still here."

"I was ten years old when we moved here from Tyler so my dad could open a branch law firm, and I always thought I wanted to go back to Tyler. But Briar Creek's not so bad. Lucas, of course, had his own agenda for wanting to return. He had quite a chip on his shoulder in those days."

"What kind of a chip?"

"Lucas hasn't had an easy life."

"I suspected that, but he won't talk about it. Every time I ask him, he changes the subject."

Tom tilted his wineglass from side to side, watching the few drops of crimson liquid glide slowly back and forth. "He's had to fight twice as hard as everybody else to get where he is today. Of course, I think his biggest stumbling block has been himself."

"What do you mean?"

"I guess it's easy enough for me to talk when my

dad's a senior partner in the law firm where I work. But I really don't think people remember the past and hold it against Lucas as much as he thinks they do.'' He shrugged. ''Or maybe they do. Like I said, it's hard for me to say.''

''What past? Why aren't his parents coming to his wedding? Why weren't they welcome in Briar Creek?''

''He'll have to tell you that.'' Tom leaned back in his chair and grinned. ''You can get it out of him. You're pretty good at playing detective.''

''Are you kidding? I can't even find out about my own past. What chance do I have of finding out about somebody else's?''

Tom's expression sobered. ''My money's on you. He'll tell you. You're a neat lady, Sara Martin, and Lucas is my best friend. I don't know what's going on between you two—''

''Nothing!'' Sara protested, tension once again shooting through her, returning to full alert all the parts of her that had become so relaxed while talking to Tom. ''Nothing's going on between Lucas and me!''

''And it's none of my business,'' Tom continued as though she hadn't spoken. ''Just be careful that both of you don't start believing you really are Analise.''

Sara smoothed her napkin in her lap, her gaze focused on her actions. Not bothering to pretend she didn't know what Tom was talking about, she nodded.

''But I have to say, I've never seen him look at Analise like—''

''Here we go, folks!'' Lucas strode into the room carrying a tray with three very chocolate-looking desserts, and Sara was left wondering about Tom's unfinished sentence...that he'd never seen Lucas look at Analise like...what?

* * *

After dinner, they sat on the patio sipping iced tea and wine, listening to the crickets and talking, the portable phone on the table a constant reminder that Lucas was an integral part of the town, a doctor on call, needed.

Parts of the conversation concerned only Tom and Lucas—the new courthouse the town was building, the plans for the annual Fourth of July picnic—and Sara felt again the sense of exclusion, of being on the outside looking in. However, they soon drifted into talk about the nation's economy, current books on the bestseller list, country music, and Sara was amazed to hear herself joining in, expressing her opinion, contributing to the conversation, as if she'd known these two men all her life, as if she belonged here.

Then Tom stood, yawned and stretched. "Guess I'd better take it home and put it to bed. I've got a busy day ahead of me." He flashed Sara a wide smile. "Calling in favors and being generally sneaky, as everybody knows lawyers are, but for a good cause this time. To help a beautiful lady." He took her hand and she rose from the lawn chair. "I promise to give it my best shot."

"Thank you," she said.

"Appreciate it, buddy." Lucas clapped Tom on the shoulder. "I'll be right back," he said to Sara then followed Tom into the house.

Sara returned to the chair, perching on the edge. Obviously she was supposed to wait. But the comfortable magic of the night was broken and she felt unsure of herself again. Should she take her leave as soon as Lucas returned or should she offer to help him with the dishes? Even though June Martin had never entertained,

Sara knew that was considered polite among the people she'd known. But did the same rule apply to the wealthy? To a single man?

Lucas returned, and she was suddenly aware that manners were not the primary cause of her nervousness. She was alone with a man who'd kissed her twice, who made her feel things she'd only read about in books…a man who was engaged to her look-alike, a man who, in spite of everything they'd been through together, was still a stranger to her.

She stood uncertainly. "Well," she began, but Lucas interrupted her.

"It's not late, and I know for a fact you have nowhere important to go tonight. The library and the bank are both closed. Would you like another glass of tea? Some wine?" He grinned, his teeth flashing white in the darkness. "Some champagne?"

She felt herself relax at his teasing. Maybe she didn't know a lot about Lucas, but, on the other hand, he really wasn't a stranger. Their peculiar relationship had forged a connection of sorts. "I was going to offer to help you clean up the kitchen."

"Oh, no. I'll stick the dishes in the dishwasher and leave the rest for the maid who comes on Wednesday."

The maid. Of course. She should have known that. Lucas was a doctor and doctors had maids.

"Well, then I'd better be going. Dinner was wonderful, and I really appreciate your enlisting Tom to help me."

He didn't answer, didn't move. His eyes, so dark they blended with the night, held hers for a long moment. She could feel his touch against her skin even though he stood several inches away. The crickets were suddenly silent, or maybe the roaring of her own blood in her ears drowned out their song.

He blinked, turned away, picked up his glass of wine and tossed down the contents, then looked upward. "I missed this when we were in Pennsylvania."

She caught her breath and followed the direction of his gaze. The stars sparkled brightly in the moonless night. "It's beautiful," she admitted.

"Yeah. They really are big and bright and the sky really is wide and high in Texas."

He was right. She'd been so caught up in her problems since she arrived, in the small sphere of her life, that she hadn't stopped to look around her. "No wonder so many songs and books are written about this state," she said quietly.

"Sit with me a few more minutes." He moved their chairs over so they'd have a view of the sky unobstructed by the tall trees that had shaded them earlier.

She nodded, sinking back into the chair as if she could sink back into that slice of easy camaraderie she'd shared earlier with Tom and Lucas.

The night air wrapped around her, warm and soft on her skin and scented with roses. Scant inches away, Lucas lounged beside her, his long legs stretched in front of him, hands crossed over his chest, his head resting on the back of the chair and turned slightly toward her so he might be looking at the stars or he might be looking at her. It was impossible to tell.

"Why did your family move to Pennsylvania? Why aren't they coming to the wedding?" It seemed the right time to ask, while darkness surrounded them, hiding their faces, turning them both into silhouettes, making their worlds the same for the moment.

He didn't move, gave no indication he'd heard her,

and she began to think she hadn't verbalized the questions after all, had thought them then given in to her shyness and kept them inside.

"My father went to prison in Huntsville." The voice was harsh. It took her a minute to comprehend that it belonged to Lucas, whose tones were always mellow and soothing like the music of a cello.

"What did he do?" she asked when it became apparent he'd finished speaking.

"He was convicted of embezzlement at the bank your pay stub came from."

"Oh. I see." She folded her hands in her lap and stared down at them. "And my coming here is stirring up old memories for you. I'm sorry."

"No!" He sounded like Lucas again, and she lifted her head to see that he was sitting upright, leaning toward her. "Sara, you can't take on the burdens of the world. And you can't stir up old memories that have never been laid to rest. If you really want to hear the whole story, I'll tell you. You're probably the only person in town who doesn't know it already."

"Yes, I'd like to hear." She recalled Tom's words that people didn't really remember the past as much as Lucas believed, but she refrained from expressing that thought.

He leaned back, again gazing up toward the sky. Abruptly he smiled. "Funny. I've spent my entire life trying to forget this story, and now you've got me dredging it up to tell the one person who hasn't heard it in sordid detail."

"You've heard mine. Yours can't be any worse."

"Probably not. Okay." He drew in a deep breath. "My father's family is Native American. The people in town didn't understand their ways and didn't trust them.

Dad had seven brothers and sisters. They all went to school here in Briar Creek, but of course they didn't fit in. They looked different, they dressed different, they thought different. When Dad was a teenager, he met my mother. Her family wasn't wealthy like Analise's, but they weren't as poor as my father's, either. Her father was a vice president at the bank. Anyway, Mom and Dad were dating secretly, and Dad wanted to take her to the prom. Openly.''

Sara wrapped her arms around herself though the night was quite warm. She knew only too well the pain of not fitting in, of wanting to belong, to escape an inherited difference.

"Even with the money Dad made working after school in the grocery store, he couldn't afford nice clothes. But he loved my mother so much, he couldn't think straight. He stole a tuxedo from a shop in Tyler. At least, he tried to steal a tuxedo. He took it in the dressing room, then put on his own clothes over it. They caught him, of course. He was seventeen, an honor student, never been in trouble before, and he swore he'd planned to return the tux after the prom, so they gave him a slap on the wrist. But everybody in town knew, and that made an already intolerable situation even worse.''

"I'm surprised your mother's parents let them marry.''

He snorted. "*Let* them? As soon as they graduated, my parents ran away and got married. They lived in Austin for a couple of years while my mom worked and my dad went to the University of Texas. He wanted to be a doctor. When my mother got pregnant with me, my grandfather begged them to move back here and he gave my dad a job in the bank.''

With his head still resting on the back of the chair, Lucas turned his face toward her. "That was the end of my dad's dream of becoming a doctor. But Mom said he never complained. He seemed to be happy. Until the day twenty-five thousand dollars turned up missing at the bank, and everything pointed to my dad. Add his youthful indiscretion to the fact that the fraudulent accounting had his signature, and nobody even questioned that, if he had wanted to steal the money, he was smart enough to do a better job of hiding it. They didn't even bring in a handwriting expert to analyze the signature. They just found him guilty and carted him off to prison."

"How did your grandfather take it?"

"To Granddad's credit, by that time he knew what my father was like, and he believed him, but it didn't matter. He was sentenced to Huntsville for ten years. Mom packed up and we moved there to be close to him. The people of Huntsville are divided into two classes. The upstanding citizens and the families of prisoners. I learned the hard way what my dad had gone through growing up."

As Lucas spoke, as he revealed the irregularities in his perfect persona, the events that had made him the person he was, Sara felt herself drawing closer to him. He'd held her body against his, kissed her lips and set her on fire, but this was touching in a different way, closeness that involved yet transcended their bodies. As she took in his words, she felt as though she was taking him inside her, that he was becoming an essential part of her. One small corner of her wanted to pull away, but the rest of her welcomed him as if he was a piece of her that had been missing and was now replaced.

"As soon as he was released, we moved to Pennsyl-

vania where nobody knew about the past. After Granddad retired, he and Grandmother moved up there to be
close to their daughter.''

''Your other grandparents, your father's parents, do
they still live here? Will they be at the wedding?''

''Yes, they still live here, and yes, they'll be at the
wedding. But I can't persuade my parents to come.
They're angry and embarrassed and stubborn.'' He
grinned wryly. ''Just as stubborn as I was about coming
back here.''

''Tom said he met you at the University of Texas in
Austin.''

''I did my undergraduate work there. When I applied
to medical school, I came to Ralph Brewster since he
had been on the board of directors at the bank when
Dad was convicted. I asked him for a recommendation
based on my college career. I know. That was a brash,
presumptuous thing for me to do, but I was still angry
about the injustices my father had suffered. I felt like
this town owed my father something.''

He sat upright and leaned forward intently. ''I was
determined to succeed where my father had failed and
to make this town accept that success. If I couldn't
make the people here see that he was innocent, I had
to at least make them accept his son. And Ralph Brewster was the first.''

''Obviously he accepted you.''

Lucas grinned. ''To my surprise, he did. Without res-
ervation. He didn't just give me a letter of recommendation. He helped me get scholarships, several of which
he established, then took me into practice with him, got
me into his country club. He told me later that he'd
always thought my father was innocent and felt guilty
that he hadn't made more of an effort to help him at

the time.'' He paused and grimaced. ''Neither of my parents could understand why I had to come back here, that I couldn't get on with the future until I'd fixed the past.''

''I understand,'' she said quietly.

He didn't move, didn't look away from her.

A dog barked somewhere in the distance and then was silent. An owl gave his eerie call.

''I know you do,'' he finally said. He half rose from his chair, as if he would come to her, touch her, pull her into his arms, hold her against him, but then he sat back, dropped his head and pressed his fingertips to his temples. ''Where do you fit into my meticulously scheduled life, Sara Martin?''

Sara flinched at the callous words that pulled her out of the false connection she'd fantasized existed with Lucas. ''I don't,'' she said, trying to make her words come out firm and uncaring instead of shaky and pain-filled. Of course she had no place in his life. She'd always known that. There was no reason for that fact to upset her.

Lucas lifted his head and looked at her then reached across the gaping chasm between them and took her hand, holding it in one of his and caressing it with the other. ''You don't believe that any more than I do.''

She swallowed hard, her mind and body swirling from the touch of his hands on hers, the warmth in his voice as he spoke. ''I don't know what to believe.''

''You can believe you're a very special person.''

The portable phone lying on the table gave a discordant ring.

Lucas dropped her hands. ''Damn! Well, I guess I should be grateful it's waited this long.''

He went to answer it. ''Lucas Daniels.'' He metamorphosed back into a doctor and left her to slowly dissolve once again into just plain Sara Martin. If that was even her name.

"Iowa? What on earth are you doing in Iowa? I thought you were in Wyoming."

Analise. The woman who might be her twin, grown from the same cluster of cells, the same blood, the same womb, bound to her more closely than any other creature on earth. The woman who had everything she'd ever wanted—loving parents, a heritage passed down for generations even if she might not have been born into it, friends who adored her...and Lucas Daniels.

"We can't do that!" Lucas shouted into the phone.

It was time for her to leave.

"Analise, you've got to come home right now! Tonight!"

Sara flinched at the edge of panic in Lucas's voice as he demanded that Analise return to him immediately. He must miss her desperately.

She moved woodenly across the patio and touched his arm. When he turned to her, she forced a smile and waved.

"What? No, wait! Don't go!" She headed for the door. "Not you...I mean...no, I don't care what kind of a wonderful surprise you're working on! Wait! No, not you! I don't care what Nick said!"

Sara closed the sliding glass door behind her and dashed through Lucas's house. The tall oak cabinets in the kitchen, the bookcases in the living room, the fireplace mantel, all seemed to loom out of the darkness, hurrying her on her way, questioning her right to be there.

As she hurried across the front yard to her car parked in the street, even the summer scent of roses was indiscernible, tucked mercifully away along with her brief, mistaken sensation of a link to Lucas.

She slid into her car, turned the key and stomped on the gas pedal. The engine cranked but didn't catch. She'd probably flooded it.

Darn!

No, make that damn! Double damn!

She turned off the ignition and held the pedal to the floor to release the excess gas, forcing herself to count slowly, to fight down the urgent need to get as far away from Lucas's house as fast as possible.

Out of the corner of her eye, she saw him emerge from the front door.

She tried again to start the car, and again it coughed and sputtered but refused to catch.

Lucas ran with long strides across the yard toward her.

With one hand she rolled up her window while she continued to crank the engine.

He tapped on her window, but she refused to look at him, concentrating instead on increasing her efforts with the car, willing it to start…while the battery slowly gave up the effort and, with a final, agonized growl, died.

Sara wanted to lay her head on the steering wheel and cry.

Instead she squared her shoulders, lifted her chin, ignored her heart beating so fast it threatened to crawl up her throat and rolled down the window. "I seem to have a problem."

Chapter Nine

"I noticed." Lucas couldn't believe how happy it made him that Sara's ancient battery had failed her. He really was losing his mind where she was concerned. What possible difference could spending a few minutes more with her make? A few more minutes to tantalize his libido, to flirt with that brain cell-destroying passion she inspired in him. "Come on back inside and I'll get my car and run you over to your motel."

They walked back to the house together, his arm occasionally, accidentally, brushing hers. It was accidentally, of course. It had to be accidentally. Surely he had a few brain cells left.

"Why did you run off so fast?" he asked, holding the door for her to enter.

"You were on a personal phone call. I didn't think—"

"Analise! I completely forgot about her. I'll be right back." He dashed through the house and out to the patio where he'd left the phone...where he'd left Analise.

The line was dead.

Carrying the phone, he walked inside to Sara as she stood quietly waiting behind the sofa, one hand resting on the back. Not committing herself by sitting. Standing alert. Ready to run. What on earth had he said to spook her so?

"Analise hung up." He returned the phone to its cradle and scowled at it. "She said she was in Iowa, getting ready to leave for Illinois, working on some grand surprise for me. Just as I laid the phone down to come after you, I thought I heard her say something about her doll."

Sara's eyes widened. "You mean Sara?"

"Yeah."

"What about her doll?"

"I don't know. I was trying to talk to you and her at the same time. She mentioned Nick again, whoever he is, and then I thought I heard her say *Sara.*"

Sara stood perfectly still, her fingers clutching the sofa so tightly her knuckles stood out starkly white against the tan color of the leather. "We moved to Iowa when I was nine and Illinois when I was fourteen."

"And you lived in Wyoming before that."

"With Nebraska and Minnesota in between."

"It's been two days since Analise was in Wyoming. That would mean one day each for Nebraska and Minnesota. It's possible, as fast as she goes."

"This is getting to be an awfully big coincidence. Do you think—" Her lips clamped shut as if she didn't dare ask the question, didn't dare hear the answer.

"Do I think she's found out about you, that she's tracking you? It could be. When she mentioned Sara, maybe she wasn't talking about her doll. Maybe her big surprise is going to be her long-lost sister." He stumbled over and sank onto the sofa. Apparently Sara was strong enough to remain standing, but that thought had sapped the strength from his legs. They'd discussed the possibility that Sara and Analise were twins, but he hadn't really accepted it. He hadn't wanted to accept it. "She insisted I had to reschedule the wedding. Perhaps so you could be there."

"This Nick she keeps talking about could be a detective." Sara's voice was soft, as if she dared not express the possibility too loudly for fear she'd frighten it away.

"Could be. I don't know what reason she'd have had to start looking, but it's possible. Analise has a way of stumbling onto information."

Sara moved slowly around the sofa and sat beside him, though with a safe distance between them.

"Did she tell you where she's staying? We have to get in touch with her. If she's looking for me, she's still got Illinois and Missouri to get through, then back here. We could save her some time."

Excitement and sadness warred on Sara's fragile features. Excitement over finding a sister and sadness because she felt the same futile attraction for him that he felt for her? She might be sitting two feet away, but it was close enough that he felt himself drawn toward her, as two magnets, unable to stay apart.

This probably wasn't the kind of long-lost-sister surprise Analise had in mind.

"No, she didn't tell me where she's staying." As he sat completely still, unable to look away from Sara's eyes, intense, pulsating heat wrapped around him. Was the air-conditioning broken? He must have left a window open. He could swear that heat brought the scent of roses.

Sara cleared her throat. "I need to get back to my motel room."

"I'll take you."

Neither of them moved.

She definitely needed to go back to her room. He needed for her to go back.

He didn't want her to go back.

He rose slowly as if moving through water and went to find his car keys.

Sara beckoned to Lucas from a field of clover dotted with sweet-smelling rosebushes. She smiled as the wind tossed her long hair and billowed her denim skirt. He started toward her but a raucous ringing stopped him.

He lifted a portable phone from underneath a rosebush and continued toward Sara, though now she seemed to be moving backward.

"You shouldn't run in slow motion like that," Analise's voice came over the phone. "You'll never be on time to get our wedding canceled."

The phone rang again. He tossed it aside and looked for Sara, but she'd disappeared.

The phone rang a third time, finally jarring Lucas from his disturbing dream.

He fumbled on the nightstand and brought the instrument to his ear, trying to wake up enough that he could comprehend whatever medical emergency might need his attention.

"I'm sorry to wake you at this hour," Ralph said, "but Clare's pretty upset. Is Analise there with you?"

"Analise? No, she's not here. I was talking to her on the phone." He rubbed his eyes and tried to clear his head. "No, that was in the dream. Earlier I was talking to her on the phone. She's in Iowa. Why is Clare upset?''

There was a long silence. "Iowa?" Ralph finally asked.

Lucas rubbed the back of his neck. "I think so."

"How did she get from Dallas to Iowa?"

"Dallas? No, it was Wyoming. Or was it Illinois?"

"Lucas, you and Analise are adults and you're about to be married. Clare and I understand if you want to, ahem, spend time together before the wedding. But you know how we worry about her. All you have to do is tell us. We just want to be sure she's all right."

"She is. She's fine." He closed one eye and focused on the digital clock. Sixteen minutes after midnight. A strange time for Ralph to call just to check on Analise.

"I'm going to ask you again, and no matter what you tell me, I'll believe you and I'm not going to be upset. Is Analise with you?"

"No, of course not."

"Did you leave her at that motel?"

That got him awake. He sat bolt upright, blinking into the darkness. "What motel? What are you talking about?"

"The Sleep Well Motel on the highway just outside town."

"No, Analise isn't there." But Sara was! What was going on?

"It was a mistake, Clare," he heard him say to his wife. "Lucas, that busybody, Sylvia Larsen, called here about an hour ago and told Clare that she'd seen you at that motel with Analise. She said the two of you were standing in front of room 112, to quote her, 'hanging all over each other.'"

Hanging all over each other? He'd stood and talked

to Sara for a few minutes! He'd never touched her. Not that he hadn't wanted to, but he'd managed to keep the lid on his seething hormones.

"I told Clare it was a case of mistaken identity, but that meddlesome woman described your car, even had the license plates."

"I swear to you, I was not at that motel with Analise." That was the truth. "Besides the fact that I have a home and don't need to go to a rented room, I would never do that. I have too much respect for Analise as well as for you and Clare."

"I know you do. In fact, I have to admit that I've been a little concerned about the lack of passion between you and Analise. Clare and I worried that maybe you two weren't so much in love with each other as comfortable, that you were getting married because everybody expected you to and because you knew how much we wanted you to."

"Oh?" Lucas ran a finger along his throat in an instinctive motion to loosen a suddenly too-tight shirt collar…except he wore only pajama bottoms.

"Not that there's anything wrong with getting married for those reasons," Ralph hurriedly assured him. "People get married for worse ones. It's just that Clare and I always wanted our little girl to have that special feeling. But I guess we just didn't see the two of you together under the right circumstances. After this past weekend, we sure won't worry about that anymore."

The invisible shirt collar was getting tighter and tighter. "You won't?" he croaked.

"The way you two looked at each other when she walked down the aisle at the rehearsal, I knew right then that somewhere along the line you'd fallen in love. And that kiss—everybody in the church could feel the sparks. Then at the rehearsal dinner, several people commented that it was like nobody else was in the room but you and Analise.''

Lucas clutched his throat again, certain he'd find a noose tightening around it by this time. At least that explained why Ralph had been looking at Sara so oddly after the rehearsal.

''I know you young people think we old fogies don't know anything about love,'' Ralph continued, ''but that's just the way it was for Clare and me. And I gotta tell you, we're thrilled for the both of you.'' He chuckled. ''Of course, now Clare's worrying about her little girl's virtue. You know Clare. She's always worrying about something. Well, you go back to sleep. I'm sorry we woke you up. I think Clare was more upset about our Analise staying in a crummy motel than about what you two might be doing in that motel. We know you're going to take good care of our baby. Good night…son.''

Lucas sat staring into the darkness until a strident beeping from the telephone he still held in one hand jerked him out of his stupor. He hung up the receiver and lay down again.

Go back to sleep? Not likely!

A turbulent storm pelted him with lightning strikes of hysteria, whirlwinds of confusion, thundering panic and basketball-size hailstones of guilt.

Ralph Brewster had described his relationship with Analise exactly. They liked each other. They were comfortable with each other. They'd been friends for so long that everybody in town expected them to get married, including Ralph and Clare. It was perfect.

He'd lived through the results of his parents' obsessive passion for each other. They'd ruined both their lives in the name of *love*.

He'd learned from their mistakes.

Now here was Ralph telling him that he wanted that destructive emotion for Analise and him. Not only wanted it for them but believed they had it!

After this past weekend.

Sara.

The way you two looked at each other when she walked down the aisle…that kiss—the sparks…the rehearsal dinner…like nobody else was in the room.

Sara.

From the first time he'd seen her, he'd known she couldn't be Analise because Analise had never turned his brain to mush while sending his hormones skyrocketing.

Even Ralph had noticed the difference.

But Ralph was wrong about him being in love with her.

Okay, he was attracted to her. *Very* attracted. And he liked her. Admired her. Respected her. Wanted to take care of her and make her happy.

But he wasn't in love.

He couldn't be in love.

He refused to be in love.

He wasn't going to disappoint Ralph and Clare and Analise.

And he wasn't going to let himself or Sara fall into the same trap his parents had fallen into.

Sara was working so hard to get her life straightened out, and he'd spent the last several years getting his together, making all the pieces fit into place. He was a happy man. Sara would be happy when she found her real family, even if all she ever found was Analise. Analise would welcome her as a sister with open arms. And Ralph and Clare, with their big hearts and abundance of love, would accept her into the family as Analise's sister, a sort of foster daughter.

Everybody would be happy as long as he didn't rock the boat. As long as he kept under lock and key that insane passion Ralph had glimpsed.

He could do that.

He flopped over and punched up his pillow.

But every time he closed his eyes, Sara's face appeared. And no matter how hard he tried to convince himself it was really Analise's face, he didn't believe himself.

Chapter Ten

Sara parked her rental car in front of her dead car and got out, determined to change her own battery rather than let Lucas do it.

When he'd come to the motel to pick her up that morning, he'd been furtive, concerned they might be seen. He told her about Ralph's call, that someone had seen them last night and thought Analise and Lucas were spending the night in the motel.

Distressed to have upset Analise's parents, Sara had agreed that they were going to have to tell Ralph and Clare the truth. Things were getting too complicated.

When they arrived at the car-rental office, Lucas had insisted he would pay for her rental, as though she didn't have the money herself. She really couldn't spare it, but that only increased her resistance to his offer. She didn't need any help, especially not his.

Even though she knew with her head that he wasn't being condescending, still she couldn't quite free her heart of June Martin's oft-repeated litany about the wide chasm between rich and poor and the impossibility of ever crossing that chasm. Even if Lucas were not engaged to Analise, Sara would never be a part of his life. The bonding she'd felt the night before on his patio had been all on her part.

When Lucas had told her that as soon as he got home that evening, he'd take her to get a battery, she hadn't argued, but she had resolved that wasn't going to happen. Their deal had been that she'd attend the wedding rehearsal and dinner and he'd introduce her to Analise and assist her in finding her mother. He had put her in touch with Tom Jenkins. Until Analise came home, she and Lucas were square. He owed her nothing.

And she darn sure—*damn* sure—didn't want to see that distant look in his eyes that had been there that morning. She was no charity case. She might be unsophisticated, a far cry from wealthy, unsure who her parents were and owned at least one dress Lucas considered *frumpy,* but she was capable of finding the hardware store and buying her own battery, thank you very much!

She lugged it over to her car and lifted the hood. Take the old one out, put the new one in. How hard could that be?

Even though she'd stayed too long at the courthouse, looking through legal documents for any clues regarding June or Albert Martin, she should still be able to get this battery changed and be on her way before Lucas came home.

For an instant her determination wavered as she thought of Lucas, of the way he'd looked at her last night as they sat on the patio after Tom left, of the things he'd told her, giving her a part of himself…of the way his lips had felt on hers the two times he'd kissed her and how hungry she was for more of his kisses.

But that wasn't going to happen. Maybe Lucas had started out in circumstances similar to hers, but he'd managed to climb out. He'd put a patch on his past and moved ahead with his new life. Even if he weren't engaged to Analise, he'd never want to return to that sort of situation. Though she hadn't needed more proof after his phone call from Analise last night, she'd seen it in his distant, detached gaze that morning.

She opened the trunk of her car and took out the tool kit her mother had insisted they always carry...just in case. *Just in case* had finally arrived.

Some time later, Sara wiped the perspiration from her forehead and expanded her newly acquired vocabulary of swearwords. This wasn't quite as easy as she'd thought. The screws were rusty and didn't want to turn. The posts had bonded with the surrounding metal and didn't want to let go. And everything she touched in the engine was covered in black grease. Actually, much of it ought to be getting close to clean by now considering how much of the grease had been transferred to her hands, arms, blouse and blue jeans.

A car turned onto the street, and she didn't have to look up to know that it was Lucas. Even if she hadn't recognized the sound of the Mercedes's engine, she could have guessed, from the way her luck had been running since she'd come to this town, that it had to be him. She bent over, trying as hard as she could to loosen the second screw. The car pulled into Lucas's driveway and stopped.

The door slammed.

"What the hell do you think you're doing?" Lucas demanded.

She jumped away from her car, startled by his angry tone. "I...I—"

"Oh, Sara! I'm sorry. I didn't recognize your, uh, I mean, I'd never seen you in jeans and I couldn't see your head for the hood. I was afraid somebody was messing with your car."

"No, I—" She shrugged and gestured to the recalcitrant battery. "I thought I could do this fast, but it's taking longer than I expected."

He grinned, then cupped her chin in his hand and tilted her face upward.

Don't touch me! her mind screamed. *Please touch me!* her body contradicted.

"Have you been using your nose to get that battery loose?" he asked. "You have grease all over your face."

She lifted one hand to her cheek, and he laughed. "Well, that took care of the last clean spot."

In spite of herself, she laughed with him.

"Let's go inside and you can get cleaned up while I change into work clothes," he suggested, taking her elbow.

He'd lost that distant look, and it would be so easy to go along with whatever he wanted, to relax and enjoy being with him. Temporarily. Until the look came back or Analise came back, whichever happened first.

"You go ahead," she said. "I'll stay out here and tinker with this."

When he returned a few minutes later wearing faded blue jeans with a denim shirt and carrying a toolbox, she'd made no more progress and gladly relinquished the job to him.

"You look nice in jeans," he said as he worked on getting the old battery out.

Nice? It was a perfectly respectable word, but she ached to hear him say something else, something less respectable. *Pretty? Attractive? Sexy?*

"Thank you." The stiffness of her reply was prompted by her own off-center feelings rather than anything Lucas had said. "They're new. My mother never let me wear them."

"Unbelievable." He emerged from under the hood. His gaze brushed slowly over her face. "You've got a whole world waiting for you to experience, and you seem to be moving into it really well."

"I do?"

"Yes, you do." He lifted out the old battery and set it on the ground then picked up the new one. "So what kind of detective work did you accomplish today?"

She caught her breath, wondering if he'd become upset with her today as he'd done yesterday when she'd told him about going to the bank. "I went to the courthouse to go through legal documents."

"That sounds like a daunting task."

She relaxed. Whatever had bothered him about her investigations into her background seemed to have vanished. "I didn't even have to lie to anybody there," she added, in case he'd disapproved of that facet. "I told the clerk I was trying to trace my family, and she showed me how to check all sorts of records. I didn't find a trace of June Martin anywhere, but I found all sorts of documents about Albert Martin. I really think my mother lied about her name. Or maybe she never even lived here."

"That's possible." His movements as he installed the battery were sure and capable, and she found it fascinating that those strong fingers now smudged with black grease, were the hands of a skilled doctor. It hadn't always been so. At one time he'd obviously learned his way around the anatomy of a car. She'd half expected to arrive and find that he'd paid someone to do the work. She liked the fact that he hadn't, that he was doing it himself.

"What did you find about Albert Martin?" he asked.

"A lot of data but nothing that really helps. He's eighty-three years old, which would make him a little old to be my father."

"He'd have been, what? Fifty-five? Fifty-six? It could be. What else?"

"His wife died twelve years ago. That's when he sold his home. They didn't have any children."

"That's interesting."

"Sharon—that's the clerk's name—she and I went to lunch together, and I finally admitted to her that I was looking for my family—adoptive, real, whatever. Her father left home when she was eight, and she hasn't seen him since. She gave me some tips her mother used to track him down for child support, but I have so little information to go on, I'm not sure I can use any of them to find more information about my adoptive mother."

Lucas slammed the hood closed and turned to her with a faint smile tracing the corners of his mouth and a wistful sadness in his eyes. "Like I said, you're moving out into the world really well. You sang at the country club. You conned the bank president into showing you records he won't show anybody else. And now you charmed someone into helping you. You've made a friend. You may have found your father. Only a few days ago when you first came here, you were too shy to do any of those things."

Sara could feel the hot blood rush to her face at Lucas's praise, at the warm tone of his voice. "But I had champagne before I sang," she explained, as if she could as easily explain away the unwanted effect he had on her. "And I did all those other things in disguise. Like you said, when I'm pretending to be somebody else, I can do things Sara Martin never could."

He leaned against her car, crossing one leg in front of the other and folding his arms over his chest. "I don't believe that. I think you have a strong spirit and it's just coming out. Your mother repressed it for a lot of years, but now you're free to find yourself. The person who sang at the country club, that bold lady, Mary Miller, who conned the bank president, they're all pieces of Sara Martin. Remember, if June Martin lied to you about your birthday, if you're Analise's twin, then you're a Leo, too, with all that fire trapped inside for all these years."

She gave a half laugh then swallowed the rest of it. Lucas wasn't laughing. He was serious.

Well, hadn't she thought last night that perhaps the lion inside was surfacing?

He straightened. "Where are your keys?"

She handed them to him and he climbed into the car. The engine roared to life with the first crank.

He got out and closed the door. "You're all set. Now come on inside and clean up and we'll call Tom. He left a message for me today, but I haven't had a chance to get back to him yet."

That got her attention. "Did he say what about?" Excitement, hope and fear all raced through her. Was she about to discover the secret of her birth? Yet, as desperately as she wanted to know, just as desperately she feared knowing.

''He didn't say, but he should be home by now. We'll find out.''

She walked beside him into the house. Thank goodness he was as grungy as she, or she wouldn't have dared enter.

He directed her to a hall bath, and she washed her face and hands. Nothing she could do about her clothes.

Back in the living room, she looked around her. She didn't dare sit anywhere. The grease might come off. But she couldn't very well stand in the middle of the floor. That would look pretty dumb. Maybe she could lean against the fireplace.

She put one hand on the mantel and tried to look casual. That didn't feel right.

One foot on the hearth, hands on the knee.

Dumb.

Just stand. Hands behind her back. Try to look casual.

''Is that a new dance, or are you allergic to all that motor oil on your clothes?''

Sara gasped and whirled to see Lucas enter the room, a wide grin stretching his lips. Blood rushed to her face. ''I was just, uh—'' Her hands fluttered vaguely as if of their own accord. ''I'm too dirty to sit.''

His gaze slowly stroked her from her feet up, his grin replaced by a hungry, almost feral look, a look that set her heart to racing. He blinked and brought back the grin, though now it seemed a little forced. ''You could be right,'' he said. ''Since I can't ask you to take off all your clothes, I'll go get you a towel.''

He left and Sara stood rooted in place, hoping he'd return soon because she really needed to sit down. *Take off all her clothes?* That thought, combined with the way he'd looked at her, conjured up all sorts of wicked, tantalizing feelings. If she had any sense of self-preservation, she'd run from the room, slide into her car with the plastic seat covers that wouldn't even flinch at all the grease she wore and drive away. Fast.

She'd do that except she wanted—needed—to hear what Tom Jenkins had to report. That was the only reason she didn't leave right now.

She'd feel one heck of a lot better if she believed that.

Lucas returned with a large, fluffy beige towel and placed it on the sofa. It almost matched. For the second time she noticed that everything in his house was neutral. How was Analise, with her room of vibrant colors and comfortable chaos, going to fit in here after they were married?

And what did it matter to her?

She marched over to the sofa and sat gingerly on the towel, tentative about soiling the plush fabric.

Without looking at her, Lucas picked up the phone and punched in a number.

She listened as he talked to Tom, as they exchanged pleasantries, then as he asked Tom to hold on while he got a pencil and paper.

That could only mean Tom had some information.

Lucas scribbled, said "uh-huh" and "I see" several times, and Sara's tension increased with every second. She found herself leaning forward, straining as if she could possibly hear what Tom was saying.

Finally, after an interminable amount of time had passed, Lucas lowered the phone, pressed the button to hang it up and turned to her. "I have good news and bad news."

Sara couldn't read anything from his expression, and she wasn't sure she was ready for either kind of news.

"Tom hasn't been able to find anything on your

mother. That is, on June Martin. Well, actually, he found that the real June Martin, the owner of that social security number, died in Los Angeles years ago.''

Sara could feel the blood drain away from her face. She clenched her fists, pushing her fingernails into her palms, concentrating on the physical pain rather than on the fact that the tiny, tenuous part of her world that had remained had just dissolved. Not only was June Martin not her mother, she wasn't even June Martin. Which meant she herself wasn't Sara Martin.

She had no name, no identity, no life. Only what she'd borrowed from Analise, and that would be coming to an abrupt end soon. She'd tell Ralph and Clare the truth. Analise would come home and marry Lucas.

And she had no idea what she would do then.

Even if Analise was her twin, she might not want a sister from nowhere. She didn't need a family. She had Ralph and Clare and Lucas.

''It looks like your mother...I mean, June...I mean—'' He plowed his fingers through his hair and let out his breath in a heavy sigh. ''Anyway, whoever she was, it would appear she assumed somebody else's identity. Probably bought it. A social security card for her and a birth certificate for you.''

She gave a shaky laugh. ''I sure hope that's the bad news.''

He smiled. ''It is. The good news is, Tom's found Albert Martin.''

Lucas watched Sara's face, waiting for her to smile, to laugh, to show some signs of excitement.

''That's wonderful,'' she said, looking and sounding more frightened than elated. He felt kind of peculiar himself, as though she was about to be taken from him when, of course, she'd never belonged to him anyway. "Where is Albert Martin?" she asked.

"Right here in town. At the Prufrock Retirement Village." He sank onto the edge of the coffee table, facing her, and offered her the portable phone. "Tom gave me Albert's number. Do you want to call him?"

"Yes," she said. "I do." But she made no move to reach for the phone. "I don't know what to say, what to tell him about who I am. I can't just blurt out everything."

Good point. "How about if you tell him your mother knew him, and you'd like to come visit him? Then you can explain the details in person."

"What if he asks who my mother was when I call him? What do I tell him then? I have no idea what her real name was."

Another good point.

Her eyes, full of questions to which he had no answers and fears he couldn't dismiss, held his. Around them the silence thickened, so complete that no sounds penetrated.

Finally she lowered her gaze to where her slender hands clutched each other in her lap. "For six months," she began, her voice soft but surprisingly firm, "ever since my mother died, I thought if I could just find out who I am, who my parents are, that I'd feel complete. I told myself it didn't matter if those parents were glad to see me or not, whether they wanted to acknowledge me or not." She lifted her head. "I was wrong. I'm not sure if I want to meet this Albert Martin. I'm not sure if I'm ready to see a total stranger and accept him as my father. I'm not sure if I'm ready for him to look at me and refuse to acknowledge me as his daughter."

"So what are you going to do?"

"Go home and think about it." She smiled ruefully. "I mean, go back to the Sleep Well Motel. That's the closest thing I've got to a home right now."

He knew what she said was true, but it didn't seem right. He wanted to deny it, to assure her—but of what? That she belonged—where? "I know how you feel," he said instead.

"I know you do. The way you felt growing up in the shadow of your father's conviction. I guess I need to do what you did, create a new life for myself and forget about the past."

"Good idea. That's exactly what you need to do." He tried to put enthusiasm into his voice, an enthusiasm he knew he should feel but didn't. What was the matter with him? Didn't he want Sara to be happy? *On her own? Without him?* Certainly that was what he wanted. "It won't hurt to hold off on contacting Albert Martin, anyway. When Analise comes back, if she's your sister, she'll want to go with you."

She bit her lip and frowned. "Analise has a life. She may not be so eager to go delving into a past that probably won't be pretty."

"Tom said he was going to check into Analise's background. Since we know who adopted her, he might be able to backtrack from her instead of you to find your identity." As he spoke, Lucas realized with a flash of dismay that he'd accepted as fact that Sara and Analise were twins. That Sara would be his sister-in-law. That being attracted to Sara, caring about her in a way that was decidedly unbrotherly, could ruin both their lives. If he married Analise—

He lifted a shaky hand to his forehead. Where had that *if* come from?

When he married Analise, he'd have to see Sara reg-

ularly. She'd have to see him regularly. He had to get
his head back on straight.

"Lucas? Are you all right?"

"Sure, I'm fine." He stood and backed away from
the sofa, from the temptation that was Sara.

She stood also. "Thank you for helping me get my
car fixed. And for getting Tom to track down my family. And for—" She shrugged and gave him a tight
smile. "Everything."

"You're welcome. No problem. Thank you for saving my hide at the wedding rehearsal."

She walked to the door and he followed, fighting the
urge to grab her, haul her back into his house, into his
life, hold her and kiss her until she knew she wasn't
alone, that she had him.

Except she didn't, of course. Not that way. She
wouldn't even want that any more than he did.

"Call me after you talk to Albert Martin," he said.

She paused in the doorway. "I will."

"And I'll call you when I hear more from Tom."

"Thanks."

"And when Analise gets back."

"Okay. Well, goodbye." She walked out the door.

"Do you want me to go with you when you meet
Albert Martin?"

Halfway across the porch, she turned back with a
smile. "I appreciate the offer, but I can handle it." She
left, walking down the sidewalk to her car, her slender
body straight, never looking around again.

She could handle it. She was doing fine, coming into
her own, blossoming. She didn't need him.

He was glad. Sara was a nice person. She deserved
to find some happiness. She'd had little enough so far.

He watched her car pull away from the curb and

fought back a sense of loneliness that threatened to swallow him.

She didn't need him.

He went inside, closed the door, turned and kicked it.

She didn't need him but he needed her. Somehow, somewhere along the way, Sara Martin had entrenched herself in his life, become important to him. And being his sister-in-law wasn't going to fill his need for her.

He ground his teeth and set his jaw. That sort of self-destructive emotion must be genetic. Apparently he'd inherited it from his parents.

Well, he wasn't going to indulge it. No way was he going to call her as soon as she got back to the motel to insist on going with her when she went to meet Albert Martin.

He checked his watch. Another ten minutes and she'd be there. He absolutely, positively was not going to pick up that phone in ten minutes and call her and ruin both their lives. He was going to break the family curse and follow his head, not his heart.

Chapter Eleven

Lucas squeezed Sara's hand as they stood in front of unit 193 of the Prufrock Retirement Village the next afternoon. "It's going to be all right, Sara."

She knew his words were meaningless, but knowing someone cared enough to say them gave her a small measure of reassurance. She drew in a deep breath and knocked, steeling herself to face whatever awaited her in the person of Albert Martin.

She'd lain awake most of the night trying unsuccessfully not to think about this meeting with Albert or about this last meeting with Lucas. After leaving his house, she'd forced herself to accept that the next time she saw him, he'd be with Analise, married to Analise. Then she got back to that anonymous motel room and answered the phone to hear his voice. When he'd said he thought he should go with her, she'd been unable to refuse the chance to be with him one more time before he became Analise's husband.

That image haunted her, distracting her from the anticipation of meeting the woman who could be her sister, invading her restless dreams with images of Lucas's wedding to a bride she first thought was her then realized was Analise.

She'd risen early, but it had taken her all morning to find the courage to call Albert Martin. In the end she hadn't told him anything except that she was a stranger in town and would like to come by to talk to him.

If she hadn't known Lucas was coming with her, she wasn't sure she could have done it.

The door to 193 opened.

For a moment she could see nothing in the comparative dimness inside, then, as her eyes adapted, she saw a short, wizened man with thin white hair.

"I'm Sara," she said. "I called you earlier. And this is Lucas Daniels, a friend."

He smiled. "Come in, Sara and Lucas. My, aren't you a pretty little thing with all that red hair. If you're selling something, I have to tell you up front I don't have any money, but you all are welcome to sit a spell and have a glass of iced tea with an old man."

Sara's heart opened to the man as waves of loneliness emanated from him, striking an answering chord in her. "I'm not selling anything, and I'd love a glass of tea."

He stepped aside to allow them to enter. Lucas placed a hand at the small of her back and somehow that touch transferred enough strength to her rubbery legs that she could walk inside.

The room was small with nondescript furniture, but the pictures that sat on all available surfaces gave it warmth and made it personal.

"Do you like your tea sweetened?"

"No, thank you," Sara replied.

"Me, neither," Lucas added.

Albert disappeared into the kitchen, and Sara looked more closely at the pictures.

"Some of these are really old." Lucas stood beside her, so close she could feel the warmth from his body. "Look at the clothing."

"They must be his family. How wonderful to have all these memories, all these pictures of people who share the same ancestors as you and have the same hair and nose and—" She lifted one and smiled. "Or lack of hair. Oh, look! This has to be Albert and his wife." She picked up one particularly ornate frame holding a black-and-white wedding picture. The young couple seemed to be gazing into the future rather than just into the camera lens, their eyes full of love and hope and happiness.

"That's Rose and me." Sara turned to see Albert holding a small tray with three large glasses of tea.

"She's beautiful."

Albert nodded. "That she was. Just as beautiful inside as she was outside. Have a seat."

Sara put the picture back down on the coffee table and sat on the boxy sofa with Lucas beside her, close enough to be comforting but not touching. Albert took a seat in a recliner. "Now tell me what brings a nice young couple like you all to this old folks' home."

"Oh, we're not a couple!" Sara corrected. "We're just friends. Lucas is—" She wrapped both hands around the cold glass of tea and refused to look at Lucas. "A friend," she finished lamely.

Albert peered more closely. "Aren't you that new doctor in Ralph Brewster's office?"

"Yes, I'm the *new* doctor."

"I thought I recognized you." Albert smiled and seemed to need no other explanation of Lucas's presence. Sara didn't elaborate. The story she had to tell this man was complicated enough without adding more.

She repeated the story of her adoption, ending with the fact that her father, as named on her phony birth certificate, was Albert Martin.

Albert listened politely, nodding occasionally, until she finished. Then it took a couple of seconds before everything seemed to register.

"Oh!" he finally said. "I see. You think I might be your daddy."

Sara waited tensely, trying not to hold her glass so tightly she'd crush it.

Lucas wrapped her wrist in his long fingers and she felt some of the tension leave. This was something she had to do, and he was letting her handle it her way, but she was awfully glad he'd insisted on coming along. Later, when this was over, she'd have to deal with leaving him again.

Later. One crisis at a time.

"Are you her father?" Lucas asked the question she couldn't force herself to put into words.

Albert's smile was sad. "I wish I was. I'd love to have a daughter like you. Rose and me, we always wanted children, but it never happened. If you'd been ours, we'd sure never have given you up for adoption, I promise you that." His faded eyes glistened with a sheen of tears. "I'm sorry."

"Me, too." She had to fight the urge of her own eyes to tear up. Having Albert Martin for a father wouldn't have been so bad. Instead, she still had no one…and neither did he. "Would you mind looking at a picture of my mother? Maybe you knew her and that's why she picked your name for my birth certificate. Maybe you worked with her at the bank."

Albert set his tea on the table, pushing aside a couple of picture frames to make room, then took a pair of glasses from his shirt pocket.

Sara fumbled in her purse and brought out June Martin's driver's license. "This is all I have. She refused to have any others taken."

Albert leaned forward, took the license from her and studied it for several minutes. "She sure looks familiar, but—" He shook his head and handed it back. "It's been so long. It's very possible she worked at the bank at the same time I did. I was there a lot of years. But my memory's not so good, and she would have had to be a lot younger than this picture when I knew her. We change a lot as we get older."

Sara's hand shook as she bent to retrieve the license. Every street she went down proved to be a dead end. She was still the woman with no name, no family, no identity, no one except Lucas, and he was borrowed. She'd have to return him to Analise soon.

Albert cupped her chin with one bony hand and tilted her face up. Gently turning her head from side to side, he peered closely at her through his glasses.

"You look like somebody I've met before, but I can't quite place who it is."

Sara's heart rate accelerated. "Think," she begged. "Try to remember."

"That won't work. When you get to my age, the harder you try to figure something out, the more your mind skitters around it. But don't you worry. It'll come to me sooner or later. You leave your phone number and I'll call you when it does."

"Right now I'm staying at the Sleep Well Motel, but I've got to move out of there."

"Here's my number," Lucas said, handing him a card.

Albert accepted the card, his gaze flicking from one to the other, obviously trying to figure out the relationship. "You got a job or a place to stay when you leave that motel?" he finally asked her.

"No. When I came down here, I didn't have any plans beyond finding my family."

The old man nodded slowly. "Don't you reckon you better get some plans pretty quick here?"

She shifted uncomfortably. It was obvious he meant she should get some plans with Lucas.

"Yes," she said. "I do." *Create a new life for myself and forget about the past.* That's what she'd told Lucas she needed to do, and he'd agreed. It would seem that was her only option. Maybe that new life shouldn't be in Briar Creek. She wasn't sure she could forget about Lucas if she lived so close, if she had to see him on a regular basis.

They stayed with Albert Martin for another hour, drinking tea and talking. He and Lucas discussed the town, new buildings, employment, the new mayor, but when those topics were exhausted, she and Albert shared their lives and their aloneness.

When they left, he walked out to Lucas's car with them. "You kids come back and visit anytime you want. I'd be pleased to adopt you unofficially as my daughter, Sara Martin."

Standing with the door open, ready to slide onto the car seat, Sara paused and smiled, tears again blurring her vision. "Thanks. I'd like that. Maybe we could go out to eat or to a movie or something."

"We sure could do that. And I'll let you know the minute I remember who it is you look like." He squinted in the sunlight. "I think it's the red hair. It'll come to me."

The red hair. Of course. In a town this small, he'd undoubtedly seen Analise at one time or another. That's who she looked like.

In spite of her disappointment, she smiled, leaned over and gave Albert a hug. "I know it will."

He shook hands with Lucas then went back into his little home and they got into the car to leave.

"How you doing?" Lucas asked.

She turned to him and smiled. "I'm okay. Really. Thanks for coming with me." She gazed at the closed door of unit 193. "I'm going to stay in touch with him." *Even if I leave town.*

"Yes, he's a nice person." He started the engine then glanced into the rearview mirror. "I don't believe this!"

"What?" Startled, she looked out the window and saw the familiar white Cadillac pull up beside them. "Omigosh! What do we do now?"

Lucas tunneled his fingers through his hair and shook his head. "Damned if I know."

"Analise!" Clare climbed out of the Cadillac and charged around to her side of the car. "Do you have any idea how upsetting this is to your father and me? You've never lied to us before."

Sara slunk down in the seat and prayed fervently for a small earthquake, one just big enough to create a hole for her to fall into.

"And Analise didn't lie this time," Lucas assured Clare.

Ralph came up on Lucas's side. "What's going on here, son? Two nights ago we get a call from Sylvia Larsen telling us she saw you two staying at that motel."

"Ralph, Sylvia never did tell us what *she* was doing at that motel."

Ralph stopped, closed his mouth and scowled. "No, she didn't. But that doesn't matter. Lucas, you assured us that wasn't Analise, that she was in Iowa. Yesterday, when she knew her mother would be playing bridge, she left a message with Annie that she was in Illinois, then just a couple of hours ago she called to say she was in Missouri, would be home tonight and she'd explain everything when she got here."

Sara sat erect, exchanging a startled glance with Lucas at the mention of the last two places she'd lived. Analise *was* tracking her! Analise knew they were sisters!

Ralph leaned farther into the car, moving his gaze across the seat to Sara. "But this evening Bert Davis called to say you were over here, that you've been here all afternoon! Barring teleportation, there's no way you could have been in Missouri when you called. Analise, what's going on? What are you doing here? Who were you visiting? Where have you been?"

Sara gaped in amazement at Analise's outraged parents. Certainly they had every right to be upset, but perhaps Analise's life wasn't so perfect after all if every move she made was reported to her parents by the nosy people of the town.

"Ralph, calm down," Lucas said. "There's an explanation for everything. Analise did not lie to you."

"I'd sure be interested to hear that explanation." Ralph's tone was a little off, a little shaky. Sara looked closer, at the tense muscles around his mouth, into his hazel eyes surrounded by fine lines of laughter and sorrow. A glance at Clare showed the same expressions.

The visible anger exhibited by Analise's parents was built on a bedrock of fear.

"I'm not your daughter," Sara said, unsure if her declaration would alleviate or exacerbate their problems. She couldn't lie to them anymore, couldn't pretend to be Analise and take their love, their concern, even their parental anger, under false pretenses.

Anguish spread over Clare's face. She leaned through the open window and wrapped her arms around Sara, pressing her cheek to hers. "What are you saying? Of course you're our daughter! What kind of stories have you been hearing? Did the man who lives in there tell you something?"

So it was true. Analise was adopted, too, and Clare and Ralph were afraid she was going to find out.

"No," Sara assured them. "The man who lives there didn't tell me anything." She hugged Clare back. This wasn't, after all, the time to confess that she was not Analise. She couldn't let Clare know that her daughter already knew her secret. Analise would have to tell her mother herself in her own way.

Sara would have to carry this charade through one last time. Ralph had said that Analise would be returning today. Possibly she was already at home waiting for them.

Ralph walked to the other side of the car and placed an arm around his wife's shoulders. "Come home now, sweetheart," he said to Sara, his voice sad, no longer angry. "We need to talk. You, too, Lucas. You're going to be part of the family. You should be in on this."

Clare clutched his hand, her face a heart-wrenching mixture of sadness and fear. "No-o-o-o." She drew out the short word, making it a mournful keen.

Ralph patted his wife's hand. "It'll be all right, Mother. We should have told her years ago."

Sara looked at both of them, at their expressions of deep love and concern. Ralph wanted to tell Analise she was adopted, but Clare didn't. She had a feeling Analise would be more prepared for this little talk than her parents were. By now she undoubtedly knew the truth.

"I can't go with you!" Sara protested. She couldn't have them going through the agony of confessing to the wrong person then having to do it all again.

"Why can't you come with us, baby?" Clare asked fearfully. "What's happened?"

"We have to run by my place for a minute," Lucas said smoothly. "I promise, Analise and I will be at your house later tonight."

Lucas and the real Analise. She was on her way home, coming back to reclaim her parents and her fiancé.

"Now, Mother," Ralph soothed, "we worried for so long that the kids didn't spend enough time together, that they didn't love each other enough to get married. I guess we can't complain about them spending too much time together now." He turned to Sara. "We'll be waiting up for you, sweetheart. We love you."

Sara looked down, avoiding that loving, trusting gaze, pinching the bridge of her nose between her thumb and one finger, focusing on the physical pain, on diverting her thoughts from Clare and Ralph. She couldn't let herself fall under their spell again. Coming out from under that spell, accepting that they belonged to Analise and not to her, that she had no parents, was too painful.

Analise was on her way home, and soon everything would be back to normal with her parents and with Lucas. Sara's only relationship to any of the three would be through Analise.

Lucas put the car into gear and backed away, leaving Ralph and Clare standing in the parking lot, their distress clinging to Sara like a thick fog. *It's not your parents you're leaving,* she told herself. *They wouldn't look so hurt if they knew you were a stranger and not their daughter. They'd look angry instead. Angry and betrayed.*

"It'll be okay," Lucas assured her. The words were as meaningless as when he'd expressed the same sentiment standing in front of Albert Martin's door, only this time she found no comfort in them.

Not your parents, she repeated to herself as they drove to Lucas's house. *Not your parents, not your fiancé,* over and over, like the refrain from a song. Or a dirge.

Lucas pulled into the driveway beside his house and stopped then got out and came around to open her door.

End of the line. Time to leave, to get in her own car, go back to that motel room, pack her bags, create a new life for herself and forget about the past.

A whole world awaited her, and over the last few days she'd gained enough courage that she actually felt able to tackle that world. She could move to Dallas. Bright lights, big city. They'd have libraries in Dallas, too. She could work and go back to school to get a degree in entomology. Do the things she'd always dreamed about doing.

She slid out and looked into his eyes and realized that she didn't want to do any of that. She wanted to go inside Lucas's house with him. She wanted him to hold her and kiss her and erase this feeling of aloneness, of not belonging to anybody.

She wanted to belong to Lucas.

She looked away, hoping he couldn't read her mind, couldn't see the shameful feelings she was having.

Heaven help her, she was in love with Lucas Daniels, a man she could never have. She wasn't sure when it had happened. Maybe the first time she'd seen him, when he'd looked up at her from the sidewalk, exasperation and pain so obvious in his dark eyes, after she'd brought him to his knees with her self-defense techniques. Or maybe it was that first kiss at the wedding rehearsal.

It really didn't matter when it had happened. It had, and that meant she had to leave.

A huge chunk of lead sat in Lucas's chest in place of his heart as Sara turned away from him. She looked toward her car where it sat in the street in front of his house, waiting to take her away from him.

Analise was on her way home. The masquerade was over. Sara would be his sister-in-law. He could never again kiss her the way he had at the church or in his living room. He couldn't allow himself to feel for her all the things he felt, the things he'd tried unsuccessfully to ignore.

Sara knew it, too. Even though she hadn't spoken during the drive home, he knew how she felt as surely as if he could read her mind. He could tell by the way she held her head, by the sadness in her eyes when she looked at him as she got out of the car. He could read her every movement, her every expression, as though his soul was bound to hers, as though they shared the same heart.

"Come on in and have a glass of—"

She lifted a hand to stop him. The corners of her mouth quirked upward, but it wasn't really a smile. "No more iced tea. We drank a quart with Albert Martin. Is that the national drink of Texas?''

He forced out a weak semblance of a grin, no more real than her smile. ''You've been Texanized. You're referring to it as a 'nation.''''

Even as they stood on the driveway, her presence brought the scent of roses. He knew now the fragrance came from his neighbor's perfectly mundane bushes, but he only noticed it when Sara was near, as though she opened all his senses, allowed him to see and hear and feel and smell things he'd never noticed before.

''Well,'' she said, folding her arms as if to keep herself warm in the sweltering summer evening, ''I guess I'd better be going. It's getting late.''

Too late. If he were honest, he'd have to admit that it had probably been too late the first time he met her, when he unbraided her long hair and found the act as intimate as if they'd made love on the public street.

''I guess so. Too bad about Albert Martin. That he's not your father, I mean.'' He was babbling, saying anything that came to mind to keep her there. He'd see her again, but it would be completely different. When she left tonight, they'd never again share this very special connection.

''Yes, it is too bad. He's a nice man. I don't suppose we'll ever know why my mother chose his name for my birth certificate, whether she knew him and wanted to use his name since she already had the Martin part or whether it was a completely random choice.''

''Either one is possible.''

For a moment neither spoke. A cicada in a nearby tree burst into its loud, raspy song then was silent.

Sara dropped her arms and Lucas stiffened, searching his mind frantically for something else to say even while he ordered himself to let her go. He shoved his hands into the pockets of his slacks to stop them from reaching for her, from physically restraining her from leaving.

"Has this whole town always spied on Analise like that?" she asked, and he hated the relief that flooded him, relief that she was still there if only for the moment. "Ralph and Clare mentioned two people who called them and reported seeing her."

"The town's done that as long as I've been here. Her parents are pretty protective. Everybody knows the Brewsters, and I think part of it is trying to get in good with the influential family in town by helping them keep track of their wayward daughter. Of course, everybody really likes them, too, so it's kind of a double duty."

"No wonder she likes to go away without telling anybody. My mother made me crazy with her overprotectiveness, but at least she didn't have the whole town to help her." She glanced at her watch. "Analise could arrive at any time. Do you think she'll come here first or go to her parents'?"

"She'll probably come by here first to get a report on what to expect from her parents. I've always done that for her."

"I have to leave before she gets here."

"Analise won't mind if you're here when she arrives. I'm sure you're the surprise she mentioned in the note she left for me. If you're here, that'll be kind of a reverse surprise for her." Was he out of his mind? He couldn't possibly deal with Sara being here when Analise arrived, with no time in between for him to get his head together. Yet he couldn't deal with Sara's going, either.

She shook her head, looking down, refusing to meet

his eyes. "I'm leaving town. I can't meet her right now."

Leaving town? "I don't understand. I thought you wanted to meet her, to find your sister."

She lifted her gaze, and her eyes were filled with agony. "I can't explain. I just have to leave. I have to make my own life before I can come back and ask to be a part of Analise's."

He knew her so well, he knew that was only a partial truth. He sensed that she felt the same way he did. She could no more deal with the role of sister-in-law than he could.

"Oh, Sara." He lifted his arms to enfold her, to share her pain. But she flinched backward, and he dropped his arms. He couldn't touch her. He didn't dare.

He wanted to tell her he loved her, but he didn't dare do that, either.

With the force of a roaring, destructive tornado, he realized that he did love her. In that wild, passionate, throw-everything-to-the-wind way he'd always feared. She stood only inches away from him, but it might as well have been miles. She was so beautiful, so clean and fresh in her white cotton blouse and blue jeans, and his life was going to be an empty shell without her.

"I have to marry Analise." His monotone assertion was directed more to himself than to her.

"I know."

"I wish—" He stopped himself from verbalizing what was in his heart. He couldn't stand to hear the words, to give them voice and make them real. "I can't hurt people," he said instead. "Analise, Clare, Ralph...you. I care for you, Sara. I care so much." What an understatement! "I'd do anything in my power to make you happy."

"I know," she repeated quietly.

"Do you? Do you know how badly I want to hold you right now and for the rest of my life? Do you know how this whole situation is ripping my guts out?" He took a step backward, again shoving his hands deep into his pockets, preventing himself from grabbing her, clutching her to him and never being able to let her go. "My parents wrecked both their lives because they couldn't think straight. I'm not going to let that happen to us. I won't make you an outcast in this town. I won't give Analise any reason to resent you. I know how much you want to have her as a sister."

As much as he loved Sara, he might even have considered doing a hatchet job on his own life if she was anyone except Analise's sister. Damaging his own life, hurting the people he loved…that would have been bad enough. But he couldn't destroy both his life and the life of the woman he loved, just the way his father had done.

Sara nodded. "I'm moving to Dallas," she said. "Tell Analise I'll be back. I want to meet her, but I can't until I've built a life for myself." She drew in a deep breath. "I'll be back when I can overcome this…this envy I have of Analise and be happy for you and her."

"I don't want you to go."

"I don't want to go, but I have to."

"We could move to another town," he blurted out. "You and I. I could set up practice somewhere else."

Had he really said that?

The unexpected outburst brought the same shock to Sara's face that he felt.

"No," she contradicted softly. "We couldn't do that. Like you said, we can't hurt people. Analise is your fiancée and she's probably my sister. We both have obligations.''

Her refusal left him feeling relieved as well as despondent. His offer had terrified him by the depth of the emotions from which it came. The thing he most feared had happened. He loved Sara as much as his parents had loved each other, enough to ruin both their lives for the sake of that love.

Thank goodness he and Sara had more sense than to do that. And damn them both for being so sensible!

For the first time he understood the power of that kind of love. He understood why his parents had done what they'd done. The only thing he didn't understand was how he was going to live the rest of his life without Sara beside him.

''Will you let me know your address when you get settled?''

She thought for a moment, then shook her head. ''I don't think that would be a very good idea.''

''You're probably right. I'd be too tempted to buy a size nine narrow glass slipper and come looking for you.''

''No, you wouldn't. You're too honorable to do anything like that.''

Honorable? He'd always thought he was, but his need for this woman was so strong, he was no longer sure what he might be tempted to do.

Steal a tuxedo to take her to the prom?

That and more.

''Tell Ralph and Clare I'm sorry for deceiving them. They're wonderful people. They deserve the truth.''

''I'll tell them. They'll understand.''

''Goodbye, Lucas.'' She turned and walked to her car, her back ramrod straight.

He followed, using every ounce of willpower he possessed to resist the urge to beg her not to go.

She opened the door, and the movement sliced through his heart like a knife.

"Sara," he choked out.

Her face was pale, her eyes shining with tears.

He had to touch her one last time, one final embrace to remember every lonely night for the rest of his life.

He lifted his hands to her shoulders and slid them along her slender arms then around her waist, over the soft cotton of her blouse. Tentatively she placed her palms against his chest and looked up at him, trust and pain and love mingling on her open face. The scent of roses wafted through the evening air and twined around them.

The muscles in his arms twitched with the effort to control himself, to refrain from pulling her against him, holding her tightly for eternity. He laid his forehead against hers instead.

"I love you, Sara," he whispered.

"I love you, Lucas." Her words were soft rose petals brushing his face and his heart, then withering and falling away as she left him.

He stood in the street and watched her until her car turned the corner and she was gone, disappearing into the dusk of the summer evening.

As he walked back to his house, he noticed that he could no longer smell his neighbor's roses. In fact, the Texas heat no longer wrapped its suffocating veil around him nor, when he went inside, did he notice the welcome cool of air-conditioning.

He was numb.

Sara had gone, taking with her every part of him that

could feel and enjoy and experience life…every part of him that mattered.

He closed the door and went to sit on the sofa where she'd sat only yesterday, hoping to catch some lingering essence of her, the fragrance of magnolias or roses or Sara.

There was none.

The sofa, like the rest of his world, was neither warm nor cold…just empty.

Chapter Twelve

The dusk surrounding Lucas deepened with a darkness that could have come in from the night outside or could have come out from inside his soul. As the darkness crept in, an understanding of his parents' sacrifices crept into his heart. Nothing mattered without love. Any pain, any humiliation, any deprivation could be borne as long as two people had love, and without it, life had no meaning, no light.

He couldn't marry Analise because they didn't have that love for each other. It wasn't a question of not hurting her. He'd be hurting her worse if he married her. Because he cared about Analise, loved her as a friend, he had to call off the engagement and leave her free to find that kind of love.

Sara had said she loved him, too, but he'd let her leave. Rather than saving both of them from the problems loving each other would bring, he'd condemned both of them to emptiness. Suddenly he knew he had to find her, catch her before she disappeared into the anonymous crowds in Dallas.

He straightened, blinking away the confusion and trying to determine how much time he'd wasted. Too much.

He flipped on a light, snatched up the phone, punched in the number for her motel and prayed she was a slow packer. If she'd already checked out...well, if she had, he'd go to Dallas and somehow he'd find her. They were linked. He could find her in a city of millions.

The doorbell rang at the same time the motel answered and put him on hold. Whoever was at the door would just have to wait.

But the visitor was insistent, alternating the dissonant ringing with a pounding. "Lucas! I know you're in there!"

Sara!

He hung up the phone, ran across the room, flung open the door and pulled her into his arms...

And knew immediately that it was Analise he held, not Sara.

She returned his embrace with her usual enthusiasm but without that passion he'd come to know with Sara, and his heart did a nosedive back into depression.

"I'm so glad you're not mad at me," she gushed, pushing away and looking up at him. Excitement, concern and something he couldn't quite identify shone from the depths of her emerald eyes. Only someone who knew her as well as he did would have noticed the faint tightness around her mouth.

What he had to say wasn't likely to ease that tightness. He ran a hand through his hair. "Analise. We need to talk."

She darted past him and perched on the back of the sofa. "I know! I have so much to tell you!"

"Analise, we can't get married."

She tugged off her engagement ring, slipped off the sofa and ran to hand it to him. The tension around her mouth eased. "I knew you'd understand! I mean, you're my best friend and I'll always love you, and I know you love me like a friend, but not like—" She blushed and bit her lip. Analise blushed. Amazing.

"You're not going to believe everything that's happened," she continued, leaving unfinished the sentence that had made her blush. "I've got to talk fast because I haven't been home yet, and I know how Mom and Dad worry about me even though they shouldn't and now they won't have to."

"Wait a minute." He looked down at the ring in his hand. "You mean you're calling off the engagement?"

Concern creased her forehead. "Oh, dear. You are upset."

"No! I'm not upset!"

"Lucas, we don't love each other the way people should love each other when they get married. Trust me, one day you'll find somebody and you'll fall head over heels in love and it'll be the most wonderful, incredible, fantastic thing that's ever happened to you and you'll know why we can't get married—"

He grabbed her shoulders, hugged her again and laughed. "I love you, Analise! In a sisterly way," he hastily amended as her expression of concern deepened.

Relief flooded her features. "You do understand! I'm so glad!" She returned his hug. "Now, I know you're wondering why I've been traveling all around the countryside, and you wouldn't believe what some of the countryside outside Texas is like. Anyway, I had planned this to be a wedding present because I knew how much it meant to you, but now it's kind of an unwedding present—"

"Analise," he interrupted, moving away from her and moving toward the phone, "I want to hear all about your trip, but there's somebody I've got to call first, before she gets out of town."

"But Lucas, don't you want to know about this horrible woman who framed your father and ruined his life?"

Lucas stopped with his hand poised over the phone. "What did you say?"

"Nick uncovered proof that your father's innocent!" She beamed, presenting the information as the gift it was. "You see, there was this awful woman who worked at the bank at the same time your father did. Her name was Abbie Prather and she stole the money but she altered the bank records and signed your father's name, and the whole thing was so incredibly blatant anybody could have seen it, but nobody tried to find out at the time because your father had been in that trouble before with the tuxedo and everybody was ready to blame him, which is why, I'm sure, she picked him to frame and—"

Lucas placed two fingers on her lips to stem the excited flow of words. His entire world had just shifted slightly on its axis, letting everything fall into place. He smiled down at her. "Thank you. That's the most wonderful present anybody ever gave me and you're the best friend I've ever had. But you've got to stop talking long enough for me to make a very important phone call. I have to catch Sara before she leaves town."

Analise yanked his fingers away. "Sara? Not Sara Martin?"

"So you *were* tracking her!"

Her eyes widened to twice their size as Analise lifted her hands to her cheeks. "You've met my sister?"

"Then she is your sister?"

"My twin sister! Do my parents know about her?"

"No. They—"

"Oh, good! I can surprise them! She's the reason Abbie Prather stole the money. She got Sara and—"

"Wait a minute. What do you mean, Abbie Prather got Sara? Sara was raised by a woman named June Martin."

"I'm trying to tell you if you'd quit interrupting me! Abbie Prather took the identity of June Martin after she stole that money and went to South Dakota with Sara. I can't believe you've actually met her! What do you mean you've got to catch her before she leaves town? When's she leaving? Why?"

"Tonight, right now." He skipped the *why* part, the part where he had to admit he'd been a fool.

"No! She can't do that! Stop dillydallying! Call her, quick! Don't let her get away!" She snatched up the phone and handed it to him.

"Analise, I love Sara. If I can catch her, I'm going to ask her to marry me."

Analise's eyes filled with tears and she hugged him again. "Oh, Lucas! That's so incredible! You're going to be my brother for real! Hurry and call her! I can't wait to meet my sister! My twin sister! Does she look exactly like me?"

So much your own mother can't tell you apart, he started to say, but stopped himself from bringing up the subject of her mother. Surely if Analise knew Sara was her sister, she realized they must both be adopted. Clare and Ralph would never have given up a child for adoption, so that meant they did the adopting. But Analise hadn't mentioned it, and he didn't want to be the one to bring it up.

"Yes, she looks exactly like you," he said, then punched in the number for the Sleep Well Motel. "Room 112," he requested when the manager finally answered.

"One-twelve checked out about ten minutes ago."

Once more Lucas plunged into despair. "Are you sure?"

"What's the matter?" Analise asked.

"She checked out ten minutes ago."

"Where's she going? Back to Deauxville? That's the small town in Missouri where she last lived, but you probably know that already. Don't worry. We can find her. I'll call Nick. He can find anyone. He's a brilliant detective."

"No, she's not going to Deauxville. She's going to Dallas—" He gave only a passing thought to *Nick*. Apparently Analise had her own story to tell, but before he could listen, he had to catch Sara. "So she'll be taking Highway 20 west. Did you drive here in your car?"

"Of course I drove in my car. Oh, I see! You bet we can catch her! Come on!" She pulled her keys from her bag and darted toward the door.

Lucas moved between her and the door. "No. I have to do this myself. Can I borrow your car?"

"Oh, Lucas, you can't drive as fast as I can! I'll drive and you look. I have to be there! I've tracked my sister all over the country, and I can't wait to meet her in person!"

He held out a hand for the keys. "Trust me, desperation will make a race-car driver out of me. And I promise to bring Sara back immediately, but I have to do this one alone.''

She relinquished the keys and gave him a wide smile. ''Okay, but just remember, gas pedal on the floor, brake pedal in the air.''

Lucas charged out the door, down the sidewalk and into the little red sports car he'd maligned so many times.

''Drive like the wind, Lucas!'' Analise called after him, and he grinned at her paraphrasing of the silly cliché.

He pulled away from the house with a screeching of tires. As he rounded a corner without slowing, he was relieved that all four tires stayed firmly on the road.

Driving as fast as he dared, Lucas headed for the highway. If he hit a radar trap and got his first speeding ticket, so be it. Sara was worth it.

Highway 20 west stretched ahead of Sara. In the darkness she couldn't see any of the lush countryside she knew surrounded her, only the small area of concrete illuminated by her headlights. That big, wide world she was entering didn't exist. Her entire world was defined by those headlights. All around her the desolate black night threatened to close in.

By now Analise was probably home, back in the bosom of her family, the arms of her fiancé.

She fought back the tears at that picture. June Martin, or whoever she was, had been right about one thing. There could be no blending between people like her and people like Lucas. Lucas loved her. He'd said so. But that wasn't enough.

She admired his attitude, his determination not to hurt anybody. In fact, that made her love him all the more.

Which only lent jagged teeth to that sharp pain in the middle of her chest.

Bright lights appeared in her rearview mirror, blinding her, and she flipped it to the night-vision side.

Repressing a sigh, she returned her attention to the road ahead, to the life ahead of her. She was leaving Briar Creek with exactly what she'd arrived with. Actually, a little more that what she'd arrived with. She'd gained a measure of self-confidence, enough to build on.

When she'd come to town, she'd had no family, so there was no reason to feel as though she'd lost something—Ralph and Clare who'd never been her parents anyway; Analise, a sister whom she'd never met; and Lucas. She had met Lucas. Had held him in her arms and felt his lips on hers. He'd whispered, *I love you,* and she'd repeated the words back to him. Even so, she'd never had him, so she couldn't lose him.

The car behind her began to honk.

What was the matter with the jerk? True, she was driving several miles below the speed limit, but she was on the right side. He could easily pass in the left lane. There were no other cars in sight.

Let him honk if that made him feel better. The disturbance outside didn't even begin to compare with the disturbance inside her heart. Would she ever forget Lucas, stop loving him, be able to come back to Briar Creek and establish a relationship with Analise? She hoped that would happen someday, but right now, she couldn't imagine it.

The creep in the car behind her pulled alongside, honking wildly, sending an uneasy feeling through Sara. Was this one of those maniacs she heard about who went around killing people on the highway for no reason?

She hit the gas to try to outrun him.

To no avail.

The car, low and fast, easily peeled around her, then moved directly in front of her. The driver motioned through the open window, pointing over the top of his car toward the shoulder of the road. Did he think she was dumb enough to voluntarily pull over?

Her heart began to race, but she ordered herself to stay calm, to assess the situation and decide how best to handle it. She could thank June Martin for one thing…the paranoia that had resulted in all that self-defense training.

She could see only one head in the small sports car. The small red sports car. That image tickled the corners of her mind, but the growing panic crowded out all thoughts except survival.

One man in the car. She could handle one man. She'd brought Lucas to his knees.

However, Lucas hadn't meant her any harm, and he hadn't been carrying a weapon. The driver in front of her could have an arsenal in that little car.

Steering with one hand, she found her purse with the other and fumbled until she located her pepper spray. Just in case.

Her fingers shook so badly, she hoped she'd be able to use it if she had to.

She saw an exit sign. Waiting until the last possible minute, she slammed on the brakes and yanked the wheel around, skidding down the exit, letting the vehicle ahead keep going.

But even before she reached the end of the ramp, she heard the squeal of tires. Was the man going to turn around and come after her, heading the wrong way? He must be insane! Thank goodness there was no traffic and he couldn't cause a wreck!

She peered closely at her options up ahead. No gas station or convenience store offered a safe haven, nothing but an empty road leading to an isolated countryside she didn't want to travel down with this maniac chasing her.

Heart hammering painfully against her ribs, she braked to a halt and scrambled out, leaving the lights on, the window open and her purse in plain view in case robbery was the only motive. Clutching her pepper spray in one hand and her car keys in the other, she ran a few feet into the dense thicket of trees and brush along the roadside. Squatting in the tall weeds, she waited, trying to calm her pounding heart and raspy breathing so he wouldn't hear her.

A split second later the red sports car whizzed down the ramp and came to a screeching halt behind her car.

Sara crouched low to the ground, straining to hear approaching footsteps over the pounding of her own blood in her ears. The dreaded sound came, a crunching as of someone moving through the underbrush. She drew in a deep, ragged breath and poised her finger on the button of the pepper spray, ready to kick, stomp, spray and run.

"Sara! Where are you? It's Lucas! Sara!"

The shock sent Sara shooting up from her hiding place. "Lucas?"

Lucas, only a couple of feet away, swung one hand in front of his face and grabbed his groin with the other. "Don't do it, Sara! It's me!"

A mixture of hysterical laughter and sobs erupted unexpectedly as her fear drained, leaving her so weak she sank back into the weeds.

Lucas leaned over her, gently lifting her to her feet and taking the pepper spray from her, then pulling her into his arms.

"Oh, sweetheart," he soothed, "I'm sorry. I didn't mean to scare you. I thought you knew it was me!"

His arms around her, his body against her, felt so good. Letting go, knowing she didn't have to fight for her life, felt so good. She wanted to stay there forever, crying and laughing on Lucas's chest, inhaling his masculine scent, his knit shirt soft against her cheek.

Of course she couldn't stay there.

Lifting her head to meet his gaze, she tried to push away from him. He relaxed his grip but didn't release her.

"That's Analise's car, isn't it?" she asked. "The red sports car."

"Yeah. I needed a fast car so I could catch you."

"So Analise is home?"

He smiled. "She's home, and everything's fine. Let's get out of this mess before we're covered with chiggers and ticks." As they made their way back to the road, Lucas kept his arm tightly around her waist. "Analise jilted me," he said. Actually, he almost sang it.

"Oh, I'm so sorry, Lucas!"

They stepped onto the asphalt surface, and Lucas took her shoulders, gently turning her to face him. "I'm not sorry. I'm happy that I don't have to hurt her. Just before she arrived, I tried to call your motel. I realized I couldn't go through with marrying her, that it wouldn't be fair to her. I love you so much, I'd steal a tuxedo to take you to a prom. I'd go to prison for you. I love the Sara who's so shy she blushes and the Sara who can con a bank president and the Sara who can sing at the country club. Whether you realize it yet or not, they're all a part of you, and I love all of you. No matter how bad things might get, nothing could be worse than not having you. Marry me, Sara. Celebrate the good times with me and make the bad ones bearable.''

Sara gaped at Lucas in astonishment. Had she actually heard right? Was he proposing to her? "M-marry you?''

"Yeah, it's what people do when they're in love. You said you love me. You do, don't you, Sara? I couldn't stand it if you didn't.''

"Y-yes,'' she stammered, happiness, disbelief and confusion mingling with the adrenaline left over from her fright, and all swirling dizzily around her. "I do love you.''

"Then it's settled. And this time my mom and dad will be able to come to the wedding.''

"They will?''

He laughed, lifting his face to the star-studded sky. "I am the happiest man alive. The woman I love is going to be my wife, and her sister, my friend, has not only given us her blessing, she's brought me the best unengagement present a man could have. Proof of my father's innocence.''

"Oh, Lucas! That's wonderful!''

"Yes, it is. I left so fast, I didn't get any details, but she said that Nick guy she kept talking about is a private detective and he discovered that Abbie Prather, alias June Martin, actually stole the money and framed my father.''

Sara's blood went cold. "June Martin? My mother stole the money and framed your father?''

Lucas swiped a hand across his forehead. "Oh, Sara! What a selfish idiot I am. I'm sorry. I was so excited, I didn't stop to think how upset you'd be to know the woman who raised you is a thief. But she's dead, Sara. The authorities can't do anything to her now."

Sara backed away from him, gently removing his hand from her waist. "No, the authorities can't do anything to my mother, but you've just cleared your family name after all those years of disgrace. You can't marry the daughter of the woman who actually committed the crime. That'll put you right where you were before."

He shook his head but made no move toward her. "No, it won't. I can never again be in that place of anger and resentment, not if I have your love. My parents were right. Nothing else matters. I used to think they were pretending that all the problems didn't bother them, that they were pretending to be happy. But they weren't. As long as we love each other, we can handle everything else."

She wanted desperately to believe him, to fall into the arms he opened to her, but she knew it couldn't be. "I don't fit in at your country club. I don't know how to make small talk or when to stop drinking champagne or even which fork to use."

"You do just fine with small talk, I don't care how much champagne you drink and you can learn which fork to use. But I could never learn to live without you. Now which one of us do you think has the biggest problem?" He smiled, and she could no longer fight the yearning in her heart.

"You," she said, moving slowly into his embrace. "You have the biggest problem because I'll never let you out of our engagement the way Analise did."

"You'll never get the chance." He pulled her to him, then hesitated. "Do you smell roses?"

"Now that you mention it, I do. There must be a patch of wild ones around somewhere."

"Maybe. But not necessarily," he said enigmatically. Before she could ask what he meant, his lips descended to hers, erasing that question and all other thoughts from her mind.

As she relaxed, giving her heart and soul into Lucas's keeping, Sara knew she'd found her family and her home and her big, wide world all in one wonderful man.

It didn't matter how many bad times were in the past. The good times stretched ahead as far as the heart could see.

Chapter Thirteen

Sara pulled up in front of Lucas's house, parking behind Analise's little red car, which Lucas had parked behind a dark blue sport-utility vehicle she'd never seen before.

After the ecstasy of her reunion with Lucas, she'd had the entire drive back to Briar Creek to worry and fret about meeting Analise who was, after all, a stranger.

Lucas climbed out and came around to open her door.

"What if Analise doesn't like me?"

"She'll love you. How could she not?"

"I don't know. I'm just so nervous. Maybe I should go back to the motel and we should wait until tomorrow for me to meet her."

"She'd have my head on a platter. I promised to bring you right back as soon as you accepted my proposal."

The door of his house flew open, spilling golden light onto the lawn, and a woman with red hair sailed out, waving her arms wildly. "Is that my sister? Is that you, Sara? Omigosh, I can't believe this!"

Before Sara could protest or worry any further, Analise enveloped her in an exuberant hug, then drew back to look at her. "This is unreal! You look just like me only prettier."

Sara felt tears in her eyes again, but tears of happiness this time. She reached up and touched Analise's cheek. "My sister," she said, her voice soft at the wonder of it all.

Analise nodded, her own eyes suspiciously bright. "I always knew you were out there. I even have a doll named Sara."

Sara laughed. "I know. I had a doll named Analise."

"I know!" Analise hooked her arm through Sara's like two schoolgirls. Two sisters. "We have so much time to make up for! Come inside so we can talk."

Lucas took her other arm, and Sara thought surely her heart would explode from being so full of love.

"I called Mom and Dad," Analise said, "and they're on their way over."

Sara stopped, pulling Analise up short. "Analise, do you know about our real parents?"

Analise smiled gently. "Yes," she said, and it was the first calm word she'd spoken since they'd met. "I know about our real parents. You mean you don't?"

"No, I don't, and it doesn't matter anymore. I have all the family I need. Lucas and I are getting married and I've found my sister."

But it did matter in spite of her brave words. Though the need to find her mother was no longer an obsession, she still wanted to know why she and Analise had been given into the care of strangers.

Analise had called her parents, Ralph and Clare, and

they were on their way. She'd have to confess her deception to those wonderful people, have to admit she wasn't their daughter and had taken their love by deceit.

Analise hugged her again. "I'm so sorry you had to go through all that bad stuff, but from now on, everything's going to be wonderful! I promise!"

As they stepped onto the front porch, a tall, masculine silhouette appeared in the lighted doorway.

"That's Nick!" Analise exclaimed. "Oh, my sweet sister, Sara! Have I ever got a story to tell you!"

"I can't wait to hear it," Sara said, smiling first at her sister then at her future husband. She'd come to Texas looking for her past. Instead she'd found a future more wonderful than she'd ever dared to dream of.

*   *   *   *   *

Find out what else happens to Sally Carleen's
ON THE WAY TO A WEDDING
in Analise's story,
A GIFT FOR THE GROOM.
Available next month
only in Silhouette Romance.

If you enjoyed what you just read,
then we've got an offer you can't resist!

Take 2 bestselling
love stories FREE!
Plus get a FREE surprise gift!

Clip this page and mail it to Silhouette Reader Service™

IN U.S.A.	**IN CANADA**
3010 Walden Ave.	P.O. Box 609
P.O. Box 1867	Fort Erie, Ontario
Buffalo, N.Y. 14240-1867	L2A 5X3

YES! Please send me 2 free Silhouette Romance® novels and my free surprise gift. Then send me 6 brand-new novels every month, which I will receive months before they're available in stores. In the U.S.A., bill me at the bargain price of $2.90 plus 25¢ delivery per book and applicable sales tax, if any*. In Canada, bill me at the bargain price of $3.25 plus 25¢ delivery per book and applicable taxes**. That's the complete price and a savings of over 10% off the cover prices—what a great deal! I understand that accepting the 2 free books and gift places me under no obligation ever to buy any books. I can always return a shipment and cancel at any time. Even if I never buy another book from Silhouette, the 2 free books and gift are mine to keep forever. So why not take us up on our invitation. You'll be glad you did!

215 SEN CNE7
315 SEN CNE9

Name	(PLEASE PRINT)	
Address	Apt.#	
City	State/Prov.	Zip/Postal Code

 * Terms and prices subject to change without notice. Sales tax applicable in N.Y.
** Canadian residents will be charged applicable provincial taxes and GST.
   All orders subject to approval. Offer limited to one per household.
   ® are registered trademarks of Harlequin Enterprises Limited.

SROM99   ©1998 Harlequin Enterprises Limited

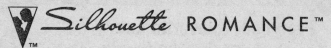

THE MACGREGORS OF OLD...

#1 *New York Times* bestselling author

NORA ROBERTS

has won readers' hearts with her enormously popular MacGregor family saga. Now read about the MacGregors' proud and passionate Scottish forebears in this romantic, tempestuous tale set against the bloody background of the historic battle of Culloden.

Coming in July 1999

REBELLION

One look at the ravishing red-haired beauty and Brigham Langston was captivated. But though Serena MacGregor had the face of an angel, she was a wildcat who spurned his advances with a rapier-sharp tongue. To hot-tempered Serena, Brigham was just another Englishman to be despised. But in the arms of the dashing and dangerous English lord, the proud Scottish beauty felt her hatred melting with the heat of their passion.

Available at your favorite retail outlet.

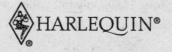

HARLEQUIN®

Coming in June 1999 from
Silhouette® Books...

Those matchmaking folks at Gulliver's Travels are at it again—and look who they're working their magic on this time, in

HOLIDAY
Honeymoons

Two Tickets to Paradise

For the first time anywhere, enjoy these two new complete stories in one sizzling volume!

HIS FIRST FATHER'S DAY   Merline Lovelace
A little girl's search for her father leads her to Tony Peretti's front door...and leads *Tony* into the arms of his long-lost love—the child's mother!

MARRIED ON THE FOURTH   Carole Buck
Can summer love turn into the real thing? When it comes to Maddy Malone and Evan Blake's Independence Day romance, the answer is a definite "yes!"

Don't miss this brand-new release—
HOLIDAY HONEYMOONS: Two Tickets to Paradise—
coming June 1999, only from Silhouette Books.

Available at your favorite retail outlet.

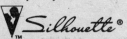

*This June 1999, the legend
continues in Jacobsville*

Diana Palmer

LONG, TALL TEXANS
EMMETT, REGAN & BURKE

This June 1999, Silhouette brings readers
an extra-special trade-size collection
for Diana Palmer's legion of fans.
These three favorite Long, Tall Texans
stories have been brought back in
one collectible trade-size edition.

*Emmett, Regan & Burke are about to be led
down the bridal path by three irresistible women.
Get ready for the fireworks!*

Don't miss this collection of favorite
Long, Tall Texans stories…
available in June 1999
at your favorite retail outlet.

Then in August 1999 watch for
LOVE WITH A LONG, TALL TEXAN
a trio of brand-new short stories featuring
three irresistible Long, Tall Texans.

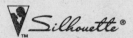